MACBETH

Other Works by Christopher Andrews

<u>Novels</u>

Pandora's Game
Paranormals
Of Wolf and Man
(Bronze IPPY winner for Horror)
Paranormals: We Are Not Alone

<u>Novelizations</u>

Hamlet: Prince of Denmark
Dream Parlor
Night of the Living Dead

<u>Collections</u>

The Darkness Within

<u>Screenplays</u>

Thirst
Dream Parlor
(written with Jonathan Lawrence)
Mistake
Vale Todo/Anything Goes
(written with Roberto Estrella)

<u>Web Series</u>

Duet

<u>Video Games</u>

Bankjob

MACBETH

A Novelization by

CHRISTOPHER ANDREWS

Adapted from the play

The Tragedy of Macbeth

by

WILLIAM SHAKESPEARE

ISBN Number: Trade Paperback #978-0-9824882-7-0

This book was printed in the United States of America.

Rising Star Visionary Press trade paperback edition: May, 2016

**A Rising Star Visionary Press book
for extra copies please contact by e-mail at
<u>risingstarvisionarypress@earthlink.net</u>
or send by regular mail to
Rising Star Visionary Press
Copies Department
P O Box 9226
Fountain Valley, CA 92728-9226**

For my wife, editor, and Imzadi,
Yvonne Isaak-Andrews,
and her endless, invaluable help and support.

For my mother,
Lynda Andrews,
whose challenges in understanding
Shakespeare inspired these works.

And for my daughter,
Arianna Andrews,
hoping she'll find this book very helpful
further along the road of her scholastic career.

WHY NOVELIZE *MACBETH*?

A FOREWORD BY THE AUTHOR

In 2005, I completed my novelization of Shakespeare's *Hamlet*. My inspiration for the novelization was triggered by my being cast in the role of Hamlet for a stage production of Tom Stoppard's *Rosencrantz and Guildenstern Are Dead*. For those unfamiliar, Stoppard took two minor characters from *Hamlet* and told the classic tale from their point of view.

Long story short: My parents, particularly my mother, could not understand Shakespeare's original language, so I rented the 1990 movie and watched it with them, "translating" the dialogue along the way.

But I discovered that, as the movie progressed, I had to do it less and less. They started "getting it" on their own. All it took was the nudge, getting past the *intimidation* of the text, and they – particularly my mother – thoroughly enjoyed the story.

How many people like my mother were out there? How many people would savor Shakespeare's works if they had a little help following the dialogue?

Too many of us only know Shakespeare from English classes, and therein lies the problem: Most English teachers assign *Macbeth* and other plays to be read as though they were a novel or essay. But plays are not meant to be read – they are meant to be *performed*. More enlightened teachers have the class read the plays aloud, which leads to far more "Ah-ha!" moments for their struggling students.

I novelized *Hamlet*, and it became my first book published by Rising Star Visionary Press. Six months later, the trade paperback was released, and not long after that, the Kindle and Nook editions. The reader response has been universally positive, with sales jumping at the beginning of the Fall and Spring semesters – I wrote the book with all readers in mind, but not surprisingly, students have been my core audience. I've received numerous flattering emails which boil down to the same request: Do more!

Hence, my novelization of Shakespeare's *Macbeth*.

As with *Hamlet*, I approached the material with a twofold goal:

(1) I would "translate" the language as little as possible, just prodding the words a bit. Sometimes this meant altering archaic terms simply because their original syntax has been lost. A few passages required additional text to identify lingo that was familiar in Shakespeare's time; some references evoked myths or folklore that were common knowledge back then, but now required a touch more explanation for today's reader. Some customs that are still present in the modern world but are not familiar worldwide, such as the royal "we" (i.e., a King referring to himself in the plural), I adjusted to avoid confusion for all readers.

But more often than not, I discovered that just flipping the subject/verb agreement or reversing what today seems like a misplaced modifier was all that was needed to make the phrase or passage clear. And other text required no alteration of any kind – once the dialogue immediately preceding and following were clarified, the original words made perfect sense with no help from me.

(2) I would elaborate within the prose as to what each character (or actor, if you will) might be doing/thinking/feeling at any given point. Thus, the dialogue would again become more clear, as the reader now has an improved context for what was being said. When it came to the Macbeth's "performance," sometimes I borrowed from Ian McKellen or Patrick Stewart or Jon Finch, but otherwise I came up with something on my own.

Because *it is all a matter of interpretation*. There are few absolutes when it comes to how a certain line should be delivered. Every actor brings something new to the role; every director has their own vision. By "acting out the story," I hope to convey what it would be like to see *Macbeth* performed, allowing the reader to better understand and enjoy the experience.

Macbeth did throw me a few curve balls that I don't recall facing in *Hamlet*:

* Different editions of the play presented different spellings of character names – Ross vs. Rosse; Mentieth vs. Menteth; Hecat vs. Heccat vs. Hecate; and so on. In these instances, I usually defaulted to whatever struck me as the simplest spelling.

* Spurious material – Many scholars question the validity of the scenes involving Hecate, the goddess whom the witches serve; some believe these scenes were taken from Thomas Middleton's *The Witch*. I opted to keep these scenes intact for this novelization, though I added footnotes identifying such passages as they occurred.

* Scene structure – Different editions integrated the

final scenes of Act V differently. If memory serves, I encountered this once in *Hamlet*, but I found it more complex here; some sources offered seven scenes for Act V, others eight, still others nine. I chose to follow the structure laid out by the Riverside Shakespeare, keeping all nine scenes separate, but again marking these with footnotes.

So here is my own interpretation of *Macbeth*. I hope both pleasure-readers and students alike will find Shakespeare's text easier to understand, but as with my adaptation of the Melancholy Dane, I *am* asking you to put your Thinking Caps on – this is still Shakespeare; I'm just sitting alongside you, as I did my parents all those years ago, to help you understand the story that much better. I've tweaked, rearranged, adjusted ... but wherever possible, I've left things completely unaltered:

> *BY THE PRICKING OF MY THUMBS,*
> *SOMETHING WICKED THIS WAY COMES.*

Some lines just demand to be left alone.

Christopher Andrews
June, 2015

Dramatis Personae

DUNCAN, King of Scotland

MALCOLM
        } Duncan's sons
DONALBAIN

MACBETH, a General in the King's army, Thane of Glamis

BANQUO, a General in the King's army

MACDUFF
      }
LENNOX
       }}
ROSS
        }}} noblemen of Scotland
MENTETH
       }}
ANGUS
      }
CATHNESS

FLEANCE, son to Banquo

SIWARD, Earl of Northumberland, General of the English forces, and Uncle to Malcolm and Donalbain

YOUNG SIWARD, his son

SEYTON, an officer attending on Macbeth

Boy, son to Macduff

An English Doctor

A Scotch Doctor

A bleeding Sergeant

A Porter

An Old Man

Three Murderers

Lady Macbeth

Lady Macduff

Gentlewoman, attending on Lady Macbeth

Hecate

Three Witches, the Weïrd Sisters, the Sisters of Fate

Three other Witches

Apparitions

Lords, Gentlemen, Officers, Soldiers, Attendants, and Messengers

LOCATIONS

Scotland; England

PART ONE

CHAPTER ONE

A desolate place. An open, hushed, lonely place.

In the distance, the sound of battle. Sword on sword; the frightened neighs of the horses; the cries of the wounded, and the dying ...

But that was elsewhere, for now. Near, but not here. Not in this place.

This dark place.

Thunder and lightning abound. As with the dissonance of combat, they were not here, not quite. And yet, their flavor marked the dominant repast. For the three sisters had come.

The Weïrd Sisters. The *witches*.

Together they huddled, clawing at the earth. Mincing abhorrent things, vile things; mincing, scattering, and, as required, eating.

The first witch, the eldest of the sisters, croaked, "When shall we three meet again? In thunder, lightning, or in rain?"

The second witch, the middle child, considered this only briefly, then stated, "When the turmoil of combat is done, when the battle is lost ... and won."

The third, the youngest, proclaimed, "That will happen before the setting of the sun."

More mincing, more scattering about ... more eating.

Then, the first: "Where shall we meet?"

The second: "Upon the heath, the open wasteland."

The third: "There to meet with Macbeth."

Across the barren expanse echoed a summons which would have chilled mortal bones to the marrow, save that only the witches could glean the beckoning of their familiars.

"I come, Graymalkin!" the first witch called to her cat.

"Paddock calls," the second witch spoke of her toad.

"Soon!" the third witch assured her great harpy.

They stood to leave and, joining hands, chanted as one:

"Fair is foul, and foul is fair:

Hover through the fog and filthy air."

Having paid toll to the forces beyond, the three sisters disappeared into the shadows.

For this is their hour, when darkness reigns.

From their camp near Forres, on the Moray coast in the north of Scotland, King Duncan surveyed the battlefield before him, and his heart sank. The trumpet call to arms promised honor and victory, with great glories that would live on in song ... but the truth was, the King felt nothing but regret and bitterness over this wasteful death. So many lives lost, Scots on both sides.

Duncan knew better than most how tenuous was the hold of the crown upon Scotland. Barely two centuries had passed since Scotland had been little more than feuding tribes, huddled together in their highlands from the reach of the Romans or the Saxons. Even now, few could appreciate the threat that England held over their sovereignty, as was evidenced by the pointless battleground before him now. Always there weighed the threat of one chieftain or another, seeking either their independence from Duncan's reign or to seize the throne for themselves.

Macdonwald was merely the latest in the long line of would-be usurpers, aye, but with the Irish supporting him from the Hebrides, the islands west of Scotland, his threat was not to be dismissed.

But though it pained Duncan to see the blood of his loyal subjects seeping into Scottish earth, there appeared to be more insurgent corpses to number. He required verification, of course, but his elder son Malcolm had promised as much to this end.

In timely fashion, Duncan was broken from his reverie by the direct approach of a grievously wounded soldier, who was nevertheless still moving under his own power.

Duncan stepped forward so that his companions – his sons, Malcolm and Donalbain, and loyal noble Lennox, as well as their ever-present attendants – should flank him. Stroking his grey beard in a manner which he believed viewed as "kingly," Duncan demanded, "What bloody man is this?" He indicated the nearing soldier even as Malcolm moved to meet the man in question. "Judging by his plight, he can report the current state of the revolt."

Malcolm confirmed that this was the very soldier for whom he had been waiting. "Father, this is the Sergeant who, like a good and hardy soldier, fought against my capture by the enemy." He greeted the wounded man, "Hail, brave friend! Say to the King your knowledge of the battle as you left it." Malcolm then offered the man his personal handkerchief, that he might staunch the blood-flow from a beastly scalp wound as he made his report.

The Sergeant accepted the offering with some reluctance, but then bowed his head in thanks as he applied it to the cut. Clearing his throat, he addressed his King.

"Doubtful the outcome stood; like two exhausted swimmers that do cling together and, in doing so, choke their skill. The merciless Macdonwald – worthy to be called a 'rebel,' for to that end the multiplying villainies of nature do swarm upon him – is supplied from the Western Isles of Scotland, with light- and heavy-armed

Irish foot soldiers; and the goddess Fortune smiled on his damned cause, appearing to our forces like a rebel's whore!" The Sergeant coughed from his sudden exertion, but then offered a smile of his own, marred somewhat by the blood on his teeth. "But they were all too weak! For brave Macbeth – and well he deserves to be called 'brave' – showed his disdain for Fortune with his brandished sword, which smoked with bloody execution, and like Valor's darling, he carved out his passage 'til he faced Macdonwald, who lacked time to shake hands or bid farewell to him, before Macbeth unseamed him from the navel to the jaws ... and fixed Macdonwald's head upon our battlements."

King Duncan was so pleased by this report of Macbeth's triumph, he clapped his hands – which prompted his supporters to follow suit. "Oh, valiant cousin!" Duncan praised Macbeth. "Worthy gentleman!"

But the Sergeant wasn't finished. "But as the shipwrecking storms and direful thunders break when the sun begins shining in Spring ... so, too, from that very Spring from whence comfort seemed to come, discomfort swells. Mark, my King of Scotland, mark ..."

Duncan frowned, resisting the temptation to silence the soldier before he could deliver bad tidings so close to the clutches of apparent victory. But denial was not a trait Duncan valued, and so he gestured for the wounded man to continue.

"No sooner had Justice, with armed valor, compelled these Irish soldiers to take to their heels, but the Norwegian Lord, spying his opportunity, began a fresh assault with furbished arms and new supplies of men."

Duncan, having heard not even a glimmer of such news, was aghast. The King of Norway had struck? Madness! "Did this not dismay our captains, Macbeth and

Banquo?"

Again, the Sergeant was showing a bloody-toothed grin. "Yes ... as sparrows dismay eagles, or the hare dismays the lion. If I say truly, I must report that Macbeth and Banquo were as cannons overcharged with double explosives, how they *doubly* redoubled strokes upon the foe! Perhaps they meant to *bathe* in their enemies' reeking wounds, or echo the slaughter of Golgatha, where Christ was crucified, I cannot tell ..."

The Sergeant looked as though he might say more, but another coughing fit left his eyes so unfocused that Malcolm stepped forward to brace the man. When he could again breathe, he bowed his head to his King.

"But I am faint," he apologized, "my gashes cry for help."

Duncan waved the soldier's regrets away. "Your words become you as well as your wounds; they both smack of honor." He turned to two of his many attendants. "Go, get him surgeons."

His attendants nodding and bowing, they rushed to escort the wounded man to the army's doctors. And before their footsteps had faded away, another party approached their camp.

Peering toward the next group of figures, Duncan again turned to Malcolm. "Who comes here?"

Malcolm recognized the newcomer and his attendants. "The worthy Thane of Ross," he gestured, deliberately using the man's title of Scottish nobility.

Lennox commented, "What a hasty look in his eyes! So should a man look that seems about to speak of strange things."

The Thane of Ross reached them, and knelt. "God save the King!"

Duncan gestured for Ross to rise. "Where did you

come from, worthy Thane?"

Regaining his feet, he replied, "From Fife, great King, where the Norwegian banners insult the sky and fan our people with cold fear. The King of Norway himself, backed with terrible numbers and assisted by that most disloyal *traitor*, the Thane of Cawdor, began an ominous conflict ... 'til the war goddess Bellona's bridegroom, our great Macbeth, clad in battle-tested armor, confronted Norway with valor to match his own – point against point, rebellious arm against arm – curbing Norway's insolent spirit ..." Ross paused, and then proudly added, "and, to conclude, the victory fell on *us*."

Lifting his arms in exultation, Duncan cried, "Great happiness!"

Pleased to be the bearer of such good tidings, Ross continued, "Now Sweno, Norway's King, craves truce; nor would we allow him the burial of his men 'til he disbursed from the small island, Saint Colme's Inch, ten thousand dollars to our general use."

This, too, pleased the King, but Duncan's honor demanded greater satisfaction. "*No more* shall that Thane of Cawdor betray our dearest interests." He pointed out toward the field of battle. "Go pronounce his immediate death ... and greet *Macbeth* with Cawdor's former title."

Ross bowed once more. "I'll see it done."

Duncan declared to all, "What he hath lost, noble Macbeth hath won!"

CHAPTER THREE

The eldest of the Weïrd Sisters waited upon an open heath not far from Forres, listening in sexual pleasure to the rumbling of thunder. Storms always gathered when the Sisters met, and she would have it no other way. The cauldron roiled with its many foul ingredients, and the oldest witch relished the scent, hacking up a mouthful of mucus to add to its elements.

From seemingly nowhere – categorically impossible, given the openness of the heath, but this was the way of things – her two sisters appeared.

The first witch faced the second. "Where hast thou been, sister?"

The second witch held up gory intestines and raw pig flesh, quite proud of her work. "Killing swine," she crowed.

The youngest then asked of the oldest, "And where thou, sister?"

The first witch cackled. "A sailor's wife had chestnuts in her lap, and munched, and munched, and munched them. 'Give me one,' quoth I. 'Be gone, witch!' the fat-rumped scab cried." A sick, amorous grin grew across her lips as she shared, "Her husband's gone to Aleppo, master of the ship *Tiger*. But in a kitchen sieve I'll sail thither, and, shaping myself as a rat without a tail,

I'll do, I'll do, and I'll do things to him."

The second witch nodded her approval. "I'll give thee a wind to sail upon."

The first witch bowed her head. "Thou art kind."

The youngest piped up. "And I another."

The eldest then proclaimed, "I myself have all the other winds, and the very ports to which they blow, all the directions that they know in the shipman's compass. I will drain him dry as hay! Neither night nor day shall sleep hang upon his eyelids; he shall live a man accursed. Weary weeks, nine times nine, shall he dwindle, waste away and pine for relief. And though his ship cannot be lost, yet it shall be tempest-tossed!" She reached into the folds of the filthy rags that served as clothing upon her body. "Look what I have ..."

The middle sister craned forward. "Show me, show me!"

Producing the sought item, the eldest held it out for her siblings to see. "Here I have a pilot's thumb, wrecked as homeward he did come."

But before her sisters could comment upon the decomposed length of flesh, all three heads shot upward as a sound echoed across the heath – though from the air or their minds, even they could not say.

"A drum," the third witch cried, "a drum! Macbeth doth come."

The eldest returned the sailor's putrid digit to her folds, so that all three could hold hands, closing their triad. Together, they chanted:

"The Weïrd Sisters, hand in hand,
Posters of the sea and land,
Thus do go about, about:
Thrice to thine, and thrice to mine
And thrice again, to make up nine."

As they ended their intonation, the eldest squeezed her sisters' hands and leered, "Peace! The charm's wound up."

They tightened their triad, coming shoulder to shoulder, bowed heads to bowed heads, until they virtually disappeared behind the steam rising from the simmering cauldron.

From out of the gloom, two soldiers emerged, men wearing well-adorned, if also well-blemished and bloody, armor. Under normal circumstances, these men would have been accompanied by an escort – not by personal attendants, as were King Duncan and his lot, but armed enlisted men or even low-rung officers. But the two Generals of Duncan's army were taking brief advantage of their rank, shedding the trappings of their status and putting some distance between themselves and the bloody fighting they had endured in the many hours and days until this point. The two traveled to meet their King, but they traveled at their leisure and they traveled alone.

Taking in the beclouded expanse of the heath – and, indeed, looking beyond it to where he knew the wounded suffered their ministrations – Macbeth, Thane of Glamis and Lord of the great castle at Inverness, commented to his companion, "So foul and fair a day, I have never seen."

His fellow General, Banquo, grunted his agreement. "How much further is it to Forres?"

Macbeth turned to answer Banquo, and that was when he spotted the cauldron. This alone was strange and out of place, so as Banquo followed his friend's gaze, each of them placed a firm hand upon the hilt of his sword. And when, a moment later, they spied the three ragged women looming beyond it, both blades were drawn.

They stood fixed, swords at the ready, Macbeth's gaze darting about in search of possible ambush.

The women said nothing. The eldest and youngest had released hands, so that the three sisters now stood in a joined line behind the steam. They were so motionless, they might not have been among the living.

"What are these," Banquo spoke at last, taking in the women's tattered, grunge-smeared garments, their decrepit, savage faces, "so withered and so wild in their attire, they look not like the inhabitants of the Earth, and yet stand here on it?"

Macbeth shook his head; he had no idea what to make of the trio.

Banquo called across to them, "Do you live? Are you beings that a man may question?"

The middle sister released her siblings' hands, but only so that they all might raise their rights in a shushing gesture.

Banquo grunted. "You seem to understand me, by each at once laying her cracked finger upon her skinny lips." He cocked his head to one side, further evaluating them, and a caustic smirk graced his own lips. "You *seem* to be women, and yet your *beards* forbid me to interpret that you are."

If the women felt anything for his gibe, their faces did not betray it.

At length Macbeth demanded, "Speak, if you can: What are you?"

While Banquo's words had fallen as flat as the heath, Macbeth's words sent an almost erotic shudder through the trio. What *were* these dingy creatures—?

Then the women raised their hands into the air, and the one on the left, who appeared to be the oldest of the three, exclaimed, "All hail, Macbeth! Hail to thee, Thane of Glamis!"

Macbeth and Banquo shared a furtive look. How had she known his name, his status? Was this some bizarre ambush after all?

Next, the middle woman cried, "All hail, Macbeth! Hail to thee, Thane of Cawdor!"

Thane of *Cawdor*? Why would they—?

Finally, the woman on the right, the youngest, proclaimed the boldest yet, "All hail, Macbeth! Thou shalt be King hereafter!"

Now the *King*? Ridiculous rubbish. Madness!

... and yet, something about the announcement slithered like a cold worm through Macbeth's guts, a sensation both repulsive and thrilling. He retreated a step.

Banquo, for his part, stood amused. "Good sir," he chuckled at Macbeth's expense, "why do you start, and seem to fear things that do sound so pleasing?"

Macbeth said nothing, fixing his gaze upon the three strange beings beyond the cauldron.

Banquo shrugged and spoke to the women. "In the name of truth: Are you fantastical, or indeed that which you outwardly appear to be? You greet my noble partner with his present title, and with such great *prediction* of noble having and of royal hope, that he stands speechless by it. To me, you speak not." He shrugged again, this time for deliberate show. "If you can look into the seeds of time, and say which grain will grow and which will not ... speak then to *me*, who neither begs your favors nor fears your hate."

For a moment, the three women remained stock still, and Banquo could not tell if they were considering his petition or not ... then they shifted their baleful gazes from Macbeth to him.

"Hail!" called the first.

"Hail!" the second

"Hail!" the third.

The first continued, "Lesser than Macbeth, and greater."

The second, "Not so happy, yet much happier."

The third, "Thou shalt beget Kings, though thou be none." She paused a heartbeat, as if to let that sink in, then added, "So all hail, Macbeth and Banquo!"

Banquo blinked. So they knew his name as well ...

Back to the first, "Banquo and Macbeth, all hail!"

And with that, the three women made as though to drift away, away from their cauldron, away from their bewildered audience.

Finally breaking free of his bedazzlement, Macbeth strode forward until he stood directly opposite the cauldron, brandishing his sword without thought. "Stay, you imperfect speakers; tell me more," he insisted. "By my father Sinel's death, I know I am Thane of Glamis ... but how of *Cawdor*? The Thane of Cawdor lives, a prosperous gentleman. And to be *King* stands not within the prospect of belief, no more than to be Cawdor." He consciously lowered his weapon and implored, "Say from whence you possess this strange information? Or why you stop our way upon this barren heath with such prophetic greeting?" When the sisters remained silent – *were* they sisters? Yes, to compare their grisly faces, he believed they were – his ire spiked, and he raised his sword once more. "*Speak*, I command you!"

The sisters responded, but not in the way Macbeth sought.

They laughed at him. And as their shrewish mirth faded away, so did they.

Macbeth and Banquo cast about in all directions, their sense of peril again writhing through their core. But no danger was in evidence, nor were the three women. Were it not for the cauldron – which remained fixed, emitting less vapor than before – they might have believed the strange beings to have been figments of their shared imagination.

Banquo grunted. "The earth has bubbles, as the water has, and these women are of them. Whither are they vanished?"

Macbeth stared down into the cauldron, and swallowed against his rising gorge upon the sight of what stewed therein. "Into the air; and what seemed corporeal melted as breath into the wind. If only they had stayed!"

Sheathing his sword, Banquo sighed and shook his head. "Were these things we do speak about really here? Or have we eaten of the root of insanity, which takes the reason prisoner?"

After a long moment, Macbeth also returned his sword to its sheath, and turned to Banquo with a crafty gleam in his eye. "Your children shall be Kings."

Banquo chuckled. "*You* shall be King."

"And Thane of Cawdor, too!" Macbeth laughed openly. "Went it not so?"

"To the selfsame tune and words—"

The echoes of footsteps crunching toward them brought both swords whipping out once more. The gait suggested neither furtiveness nor threat, but the Generals were understandably high-strung after their otherworldly encounter.

"Who's here?" Banquo demanded.

A familiar voice eased the men back from the edge. "The King hath happily received, Macbeth, the news of your success ..."

Macbeth and Banquo exchanged a knowing, and somewhat embarrassed, look as they put away their weapons once more and joined hands with the arriving noblemen, Ross and Angus.

Ross continued, "... and when he reads of your personal venture in the rebels' fight, his astonishment and his admiration do contend which should be yours or his! Silenced by this conflict, and in viewing over the rest of the selfsame day, Duncan finds you fighting amongst the stout Norwegian ranks, never afraid of what you yourself did make – strange images of death for those you fought. Messenger after messenger came as thick as hailstones, and *every one* did bear your praises in his Kingdom's great defense, and poured them down before him."

"We are sent," Angus chimed in, "to give you thanks from our royal master – only to herald you into his sight, not pay your reward ourselves."

"*And,*" Ross continued, showing faint irritation toward Angus for the interruption, "for a pledge of a greater honor, Duncan bade me, from him, call you *Thane of Cawdor* – in which title: Hail, most worthy Thane! For it is yours." Both he and Angus bowed their heads.

Had they not done so, had they not been so caught up in the excitement of bearing such wonderful tidings, they might have noted the ashen pallor which overwhelmed Banquo and, even more so, Macbeth.

Banquo whispered to his companion. "What, can the Devil speak true?"

To Ross and Angus, Macbeth cleared his throat and insisted, "The Thane of Cawdor lives. Why do you dress me in borrowed robes?"

Angus was pleased to explain. "He who *was* the Thane lives yet, but bears that life – which he deserves to *lose* – under heavy judgement. Whether he was allied with those of Norway or did reinforce the rebel

Macdonwald with hidden help and vantage, or that he labored with *both* in his country's ruin, I know not. But treasons capital, confessed and proved, have overthrown him."

Macbeth forced his expression to remain neutral, but within, he stood awestruck. *Thane of Glamis, now Thane of Cawdor! And the greatest to come.*

Clearing his throat once more, he laid his hands upon the forearms of Ross and Angus. "Thanks for your pains."

The men beamed at his appreciation, and thought nothing of it as Macbeth then stepped aside and spoke to Banquo under his breath.

"Do you not hope," Macbeth asked, "that your children shall be Kings, when those that gave the Thane of Cawdor to me promised no less to them?"

Banquo grunted, and it was not a happy sound. "That, trusted to the utmost, might yet offer *you* hopes for the crown, besides the Thane of Cawdor." He glanced toward the cooling cauldron, the fires beneath having died out. "But it is a strange business. And oftentimes, to woo us toward our own harm, the instruments of darkness tell us truths, win us with honest trivialities ... to then *betray* us in matters of greater importance." Shuddering, wishing to distance himself from these thoughts, Banquo spat toward the cauldron, turned on his heel, and approached Ross and Angus with a raised voice. "Fellow Lords, a word, I pray you."

Macbeth, for his part, held his gaze upon the cauldron. *Two truths are told, as happy prologues to the stately act of my imperial theme.*

A moment later, Macbeth realized that the others had presumed his joining Banquo, as all three men looked toward him, expectant. He smiled and gestured to Ross and Angus, stating, "I thank you, gentlemen." He then deliberately turned his back and drifted a few steps away, making it clear that he sought a few moments of privacy.

In particular, he wanted to avoid Banquo, did not want his friend to glean the look in his eye, lest he decipher to which direction Macbeth's musings flowed.

This supernatural temptation, his thoughts continued, *cannot be ill, nor cannot be good. If ill, why has it predicted my earnest success, which commenced to be true? I am Thane of Cawdor. But ... if good ... why am I allured by that suggestion – whose horrid image does unfix my hair and make my seated heart knock at my ribs – against the custom of nature, to* kill *my* King? Macbeth closed his eyes. *Fears of the here and now are less frightening than these horrible imaginings! My thoughts, where murder is nothing yet but fantastical, so shakes my mortal constitution that normal function is smothered in speculation, and nothing matters but what is not yet real.*

Striving to keep his comment light – both for his fellow noblemen, as well as himself – Banquo gestured toward the brooding Macbeth and remarked, "Look, how our partner is rapt." He said it loudly and with forced mirth, intending Macbeth to overhear and be jarred from his daze.

Perhaps some part of Macbeth heard it, for though he did not outwardly respond, he strove to shake himself loose from these traitorous wonderings. What were these treasonable notions, of *killing* Scotland's monarch? Prompted by the wild predictions of three deranged women – if women they were – he contemplated regicide? As a General and a Thane twice over, he of all should stand better! Why, had he not just shed oceans of blood in defense of that crown?

Still ... it was a violent world, an unjust world. He

was Duncan's cousin, and well honored by his countrymen. Perhaps the sisters' prophetic proclamations would prove true, in time – *without* the wanton betrayal of his own action!

If chance will have me King ... why, chance may crown me, without my *initiative.*

"New honors come upon him with this title of Cawdor," Banquo continued, still with strained good humor, "which, like unfamiliar garments, cleave not to their owner's shape but with the aid of usage and time."

Come what may, Macbeth concluded, *time and the hour runs through the roughest day.*

At the wit's end of subtlety, Banquo cut to the chase and addressed him directly. "Worthy Macbeth, we only stay upon your leisure."

Finally snapping free of his uncomfortable contemplation, Macbeth scoffed at himself. "Give me your pardon! My dull brain was troubled with things forgotten." To Ross and Angus, he said, "But, kind gentlemen, the pains you have taken for me are registered in my memory where, every day, I shall turn the leaf to read them. Let us go toward the King."

But even as Ross and Angus began their march, Macbeth placed his hand upon Banquo's arm, slowing him so that – although they continued after the other noblemen – within a few strides, they had some privacy.

"Think upon what has happened this day," Macbeth said in a low voice, "and, at a more opportune time, having weighed it in the interim, let us speak our thoughts freely, each to the other."

Banquo grunted. "Very gladly."

"Until then, enough." The others had noted his and Banquo's lingering, so he increased his stride until he surpassed them. "Come, friends!"

And as the quartet departed the heath, Macbeth almost fooled himself into believing that he took no note of the cauldron's exact location, might he have reason to return here at another time.

Almost ...

PART ONE

CHAPTER FOUR

The palace at Forres: The present seat of the throne of Scotland, its battlements rose high, its proud banners higher still. Those who visited its stone walls could shut out the troubles of the land, push from their minds the insipid uprisings of the chieftains, and feign confidence – to themselves and to others – that Scotland stood on the edge of greatness, that Duncan would, somehow, usher them unto an empire of their very own.

With a flourish of trumpets, King Duncan entered the throne room, trailed by his sons, Malcolm and Donalbain, who were in turn followed by Lennox and their collective band of attendants.

"Is the execution done on the former Thane of Cawdor?" Duncan asked his elder son as he strode toward his wooden, but elegantly carved, throne, stroking his grey beard as he was wont. "Are those in commission of this duty not yet returned?"

"My liege," Malcolm replied, "they have not yet come back. But I have spoken with someone who saw him die, who did report that, very frankly, he confessed his treasons, implored Your Highness' pardon, and set forth a deep repentance." Malcolm shook his head, and added, almost to himself, "Nothing in his whole life flattered him like the *leaving* of it. He died as one who had *studied* for his death, to throw away the dearest thing he owned as if it were a meaningless trifle."

But the King had other worries. He fairly collapsed onto the throne, his weariness running deeper than his tired limbs. "There's no method to know a man's mind by looking upon his face. He was a gentleman on whom I built an absolute trust." Such treachery made him doubly grateful for Macbeth. Who else could he—?

Then Macbeth and Banquo entered the throne room, escorted by Ross and Angus, and Duncan's mood brightened a great deal.

"Oh, worthiest cousin!" the King called, rising once more, his fatigue forgotten. He spread his arms wide as he greeted Macbeth. "The sin of my ingratitude even now was heavy on me. You are so far ahead in serving me that the swiftest wing of my recompense is slow to overtake you. Were you less deserved, then the proportion both of thanks and payment might have been mine! I only have left to say, your due is more than I can ever repay."

Macbeth knelt before his King. "The service and the loyalty I owe; in doing so, it repays itself. Your Highness' part is to receive our duties; and our duties to your throne and state are like those of children to parents and servants to masters – which do nothing but what they should, and by doing *every*thing to secure your love and honor."

Duncan beamed and placed his hands upon Macbeth's shoulders, pulling him to his feet and into a warm embrace. "Welcome hither! As the new Thane of Cawdor, I have planted the seeds of your career, and will labor to make them full of growth."

He then stepped back and turned toward Banquo, who knelt as Macbeth had before him.

"Noble Banquo," the King proclaimed, "who has no

less deserved my love, nor must be known no less to have done so, let me enfold you and hold you to my heart." As with Macbeth, he pulled the man up and wrapped his arms around him.

"If there I grow," Banquo returned, "the harvest shall be your own doing."

Releasing Banquo, Duncan turned back toward his throne, raising his voice so that all could hear him speak. "My plenteous joys, unrestrained in fullness, seek to hide themselves in drops of sorrow from my eyes."

This brought amused chuckling from many in attendance, which gave time for Duncan to reach his destination. Rather than sit, however, he stood before the throne and announced to the room, "Sons, kinsmen, Thanes, and you whose places are the nearest ..."

Duncan paused, assuring that he had everyone's ear ... and Macbeth found himself disliking the sudden gleam in the King's eyes as he glanced toward Malcolm.

Duncan continued, "... know that I shall now settle the succession of my throne upon my eldest, Malcolm, whom I name hereafter the *Prince of Cumberland*!"

Applause sounded from all around, most present pleased to see the title of the Scottish heir-apparent officially bequeathed to Malcolm; he was both liked and respected across the land.

Macbeth clapped with the others, but it was a forced gesture on his part.

"Which honor must not invest Malcolm alone," Duncan concluded, spread his arms once more, "but rewards of nobleness, like stars, shall shine upon *all* deservers."

Smiles flowed back and forth like a tossed current, and Macbeth strove to hide the clenching of his jaw as the King approached him once more.

"From here we reconvene to Inverness," Duncan declared, referring to Macbeth's castle, "and oblige myself further to you by your hospitality."

Macbeth scoffed, as was expected. "Any 'rest' is *labor*, when it is not used for *you*. I'll be the harbinger myself, and make the hearing of my wife joyful with news of your approach." He bowed his head. "So I humbly take my leave."

Duncan clapped his own hands once, crying, "My worthy Cawdor!" He then turned, passing the grace of his eye to others.

Macbeth made certain his back was turned to all before allowing the gloom to lower over his face. *Malcolm, the Prince of Cumberland! That is a step on which I must falter ... or else overleap, for it lies in* my *way to the throne!*

But still, as he departed, Macbeth struggled with these thoughts, a lifetime of loyalty not to be dismissed so easily.

Stars, hide your fires; give no light to see my black and deep desires. Let the eye be blind to the hand's actions ... yet let that come to pass, which, when it is done, the eye fears to see.

Looking after Macbeth's exodus, King Duncan commented further to Banquo, "Very true, worthy Banquo! Macbeth is indeed so valiant, and in his commendations, I am fed; it is a banquet to me. Let's follow after him, who has gone ahead to bid us welcome." Duncan sighed, content in the moment, thoughts of the former Thane of Cawdor now distant. "He is a *peerless* kinsman!"

Banquo nodded his hearty agreement ... and sought to snuff out the flame of apprehension when he recalled their strange encounter upon the heath.

Part One

Chapter Five

Macbeth's castle at Inverness lacked some of the majesty of the King's, but not a great deal. Located west of Forres, it rose proudly atop a solitary mountain, an alpine outlook which would have stood comfortably among the highlands further north.

The gates were currently open, awaiting the return of its master, and the sun's rays were just beginning to golden as Lady Macbeth – she had proudly taken her husband's name on the day of their wedding, never again to be called "the Lady Gruoch" – strode out onto their private platform near the peak. She stood with her back to the wind, stealing a moment's admiration for the view, before returning her attention to the secret letter she had received from her partner and consort.

Fingering a lock of her long, dark hair, she continued reading, " 'They met me on the day of success; and I have since learned, by the perfectest report, that they have more in them than *mortal knowledge*.' "

She paused a moment at that, considered it, absorbed it.

" 'When I burned in desire to question them further ... they made themselves *air*, into which they vanished. Whiles I stood rapt in the wonder of it, messengers came from the King, who all-hailed me "*Thane of Cawdor*" – by which title, before, these Weïrd Sisters saluted me ... and next referred to me with *"Hail, King that shalt be!"* ' "

Again, Lady Macbeth stopped, taking it in. *King that shalt be!*

" 'This have I thought good to report to you, my dearest partner of greatness, that you might not lose the dues of rejoicing, by being ignorant of what greatness is promised us.

" 'Lock this secret within your heart, and farewell.' "

She folded the letter once, twice, three times, then secured it within her bodice. As her fingers brushed against her breast, she noted the intensity of her heartbeat; it did not seem, to her, to beat a great deal faster, merely *harder*, with great force.

Glamis you are, she thought to her absent husband, *and now Cawdor ... and you* shall be *what you have been promised!*

She licked her lips and dug her fingers into the stone before her, overlooking the land far below. Could this truly be possible? She loved Macbeth dearly, admired his grace and his strength ... but, deep within, it had often galled her that "Thane of Glamis" was the height of his future. An admired General, to be sure, richer than some other Thanes who, being fellow Scottish noblemen, might've been lawfully entitled to as much, but still having reached the summit of his political climb. Was he not the King's cousin? Did they not descend from a shared grandparent? Could there truly be nothing *more*?

And these uprisings! She believed they occurred, over and over, because Duncan was too weak, too delicate of personality to *will* the Scots together. She had hinted as much to Macbeth once before, and when he did not silence her disloyal attitude, she knew that he agreed with her.

But now ... *now* ... if these "Weïrd Sisters" truly had the gift of foresight, if Macbeth would be willing ...!

Yet I do fear your nature, she admitted to her mate of

her mind. *It is too full of the milk of human kindness to seize the shortest way. You desire to be great, are not without ambition, but lack the wickedness which should accompany it. What you seek most highly, you desire to achieve honestly; you will not play falsely, and yet crave that which you are not entitled to. You wish to have, great Glamis, that which cries: "This thing you must do, if you would have it ... and that which you do fear to do, you wish should be done* for *you."*

In answer to this, Lady Macbeth smiled a dark smile into the setting sun.

Hasten here, that I may pour my *spirit in your ear, and chastise with the valor of my tongue all that impedes you from the golden crown – with which fate, and supernatural aid, do seem to have crowned you!*

When the door behind her opened, she almost jolted. Had she been speaking her thoughts aloud? No, surely not. And even if she had, the wind alone would have masked her words.

She glanced over her shoulder to confirm it was one of the house messengers, then returned to gazing upon the sunset. "What are your tidings?" she asked, her tone casual.

Quite pleased to carry extraordinary news, the messenger declared, "The *King* comes here tonight!"

Lady Macbeth whirled, any aspirations of remaining "casual" shattered by this startling information. "You are *mad* to say it!"

The messenger blinked, at a loss.

Lady Macbeth noticed this, scolded herself for her lack of control, and continued in a calmer voice, "Is your master not with him? Who, were this news true, would have informed me, so that I could make with preparations?"

Treading carefully, the messenger assured her, "So please you, it *is* true; our Thane *is* coming. One of my fellows outdistanced him – a courier who, almost dead for breath, had scarcely enough to deliver his message."

Lady Macbeth nodded. "Give him tending; he brings *great* news."

The messenger, relieved to have cheered his Lady after all, snapped a quick bow and departed, closing the door behind him.

Lady Macbeth could scarcely believe this fortuitous twist of fate, bringing Duncan within her grasp on the heels of Macbeth's letter.

The raven himself is hoarse, she marveled, *that croaks the fatal entrance of Duncan under my battlements.*

She shifted her gaze, from the sun setting in the west to the first twinkling stars in the night sky of the east.

Come, you spirits that tend on murderous thoughts – unsex my womanhood here, and fill me, from crown to toe, full of direst cruelty! Make thick my blood, stop up the access and passage to remorse, so that no compunctious visitings of natural feelings shake my cruel purpose, nor intervene between my goal and its effect! Come to my woman's breasts and exchange my milk for venom, *you murdering ministers – wherever in your invisible substances you wait on nature's evil! Come, thick night, and enshroud yourself in the darkest smoke of Hell, that my keen knife does not see the wound it makes, nor Heaven peep through the blanket of the dark, to cry "Hold, hold!"*

The door opened once more, and this time she kept her head about her ... until she turned and saw who it was.

Macbeth stood framed against the corridor beyond. His hair and clothes were covered in dust, and she imagined he smelled as distasteful as he looked, but she had never been so excited to lay eyes upon him.

"Great Glamis!" she cried as she rushed to him. "Worthy *Cawdor*!" She threw her arms around his neck, and kissed him deeply.

Though weary from the road, Macbeth returned her passion ounce for ounce.

When they broke apart for mutual air, she continued, but in a softer voice, "Greater than *both*, by the 'all-hail' which followed! Your letter has transported me beyond this ignorant present, and I feel now the *future* in this instant."

Nodding absently, caressing her cheek, he replied, "My dearest love, Duncan comes here tonight."

She, too, nodded, but hurried to ask, "And when goes hence?"

"Tomorrow, as he purposes."

The dark smile returned to Lady Macbeth's lips. "Oh, *never* shall that morrow see sun!" She lifted her own hand to his cheek, but her touch was more clinical, more critical. "Your face, my Thane, is as a book where men may read strange matters. To beguile the world, *look* like the world – bear welcome in your eye, your hand, your tongue. *Look* like the innocent flower ... but *be* the serpent underneath."

She stepped away, taking him in. He appeared neither squeamish nor determined.

Putting on her courtly manner, she told him, "The King that's coming must be provided for, and you shall put this night's great business into *my* management ... which shall, to all our future nights and days to come, give solely sovereign sway and masterdom."

Still Macbeth held his noncommittal expression, but Lady Macbeth was heartened by his next words. "We will speak further."

She bowed her head with barely contained excitement. "Only look about with serenity; to alter your expression, ever, is to create fear in others." She then took his hand in her own, and her eyes glistened in the fading light. "Leave all the rest to *me*."

CHAPTER SIX

Night had nearly fallen upon the road leading up to the castle at Inverness, and many stars shone brightly in the east. But the castle itself, high upon its mount, still gleamed in the final rays of the sun.

King Duncan, surrounded by the reedy hum of hautboys and the stark relief of torches, leaned back in his saddle as they reached the castle gate. His party included Malcolm and Donalbain, Banquo, Lennox, Macduff, Ross, and Angus – and attendants, of course; always attendants – but it was Macbeth's closest comrade and friend whom he addressed.

"This castle has a pleasant seat," the King commented to Banquo as he gazed upon their destination, "the air nimbly and sweetly recommends itself to my fine senses."

Banquo grunted his agreement. "This guest of summer, the church-nesting bird – the house martin – does prove, by his loved nest-building, that Heaven's breath smells wooingly here. No jutty protrusion, decorated frieze, supporting buttress, nor convenient corner avoids this bird making his hanging bed and breeding cradle." He sighed, contented. "I have observed that where they most breed and haunt, the air is delicate."

As they passed under the gates, the hautboys

announcing their liege's arrival with extra fanfare, Duncan spied Lady Macbeth swiftly approaching them.

"See, see, our honored hostess!" he called, descending from his horse without waiting for his attendants to assist him. He held forth his arms to take her hands. "The love that follows me is sometimes my trouble, while I still appreciate this trouble *as* love. Herein I teach you how you shall bid God reward me for your pains, and thank me for *your* trouble."

Lady Macbeth both agreed and demurred as she bowed her head, "All our 'trouble,' if every point were twice done and then doubled again, would make poor and single business to attempt to match those honors – deep and broad – which Your Majesty loads upon our house. For those honors of old, and the latest dignities heaped upon them, we gratefully pray for you."

Duncan beamed at her welcome, squeezing her hands like an adoring father before releasing them. "Where's the Thane of Cawdor? We rode close upon his heels, and had intended to be his purveyor. But he rides well; and his great love for *you*, sharp as his spur, has helped him to his home before us." He then stepped back and raised his voice for all to hear. "Fair and noble hostess, I am your guest tonight."

Lady Macbeth bowed her head once more. "We, your servants, always have ours – ourselves and what is ours – in *your* royal trust, to make our accounting at Your Highness' pleasure, always to return *your own*."

The King, glowing at her selflessness in his name, reached out to her once more. "Give me your hand. Conduct me to mine host; I love him highly, and shall continue my graces towards him." And as she took his hand in hers, he gestured forward with his other. "By your leave, hostess."

Part One

Chapter Seven

Dinner was a smashing success. As the hautboys played and torches lit the banquet chamber of the inner court of the castle, butlers and servants rushed to and fro with dishes and utensils, trading out one course for the next, seeing to it that their master's honored guest received top indulgence. And as much food as was consumed, it was matched evenly by the intake of wine and stronger spirits.

Macbeth and Lady Macbeth sat on either side of their King, but while she doted upon Duncan, laughing at his jokes – and gently flirting with him as much as social intercourse would permit, and likewise expected – Macbeth found that, against his strong effort, his focus drifted ever inward ...

If it were finished when it is done, he pondered, *then it would be well if it were done quickly. If the assassination could ensnare the consequences that follow, and catch success upon his death, if this blow might be the be-all and the end-all here, in this world ... then here, upon this shallow sandbank of time, we would risk the afterlife to come.*

He glanced casually at Duncan, who drank deeply of his wine, with Lady Macbeth's encouragement.

But in these cases, we always bear judgement here,

in that we but teach bloody instructions – which, being taught, return to plague the instructors. This even-handed justice presents the ingredients of our poisoned chalice to our own lips.

Macbeth could no longer stand to look upon Duncan's smiling, relaxed face. Seizing an empty flagon of wine an instant before a faithful butler could collect it, he stood – mumbling an unintelligible apology to his King while gesturing with the flagon toward the kitchen – and left the dining table. He shuffled in the general direction of the kitchen entree, while his true destination was a private nook just beyond.

He's here in double trust, his mind raged on, *first, as I am his kinsman and his subject – both strong against the deed – then, as his* host, *who should shut the door* against *his murderer, not bear the knife myself!*

He reached the nook, stepped into the deep shadows, and leaned back against the wall, his eyes closed.

Besides, this Duncan has borne his royal authority so humbly, has been so blameless in his great office, that his virtues will plead like angels, trumpet-tongued, against the deep unjustness of his murder. And pity – like *a naked, newborn babe, bestriding the blast, or Heaven's angels, horsed upon the invisible winds of the air – shall blow word of the horrid deed into every eye, so that the masses' tears shall drown the wind like rain.* Macbeth shook his head. *I have no spur to prick the sides of my intent, but only vaulting ambition ... which overleaps itself and falls on the other side—*

A rustle of cloth caused Macbeth to jump, his eyes flying open wide, praying that the shadows might hide the guilt that surely stood in clear report upon his face ...

But he was relieved – and yet, also somehow uneasy – to find that it was his wife who had stumbled upon him.

"How now?" he asked, willing his voice to remain steady and placid. "What news?"

"Duncan has almost supped," Lady Macbeth replied, her tone not-quite-suspicious. "Why have you left the chamber?"

"Has he asked for me?"

"Do you not know he has?"

Macbeth stood staring at his wife for a long moment, considering, weighing ...

When at last he spoke, it was with a firm voice. "We will proceed no further in this business."

Lady Macbeth looked as though he had slapped her. To avoid her ferocious, aggrieved gaze, he considered the empty flagon, still in his hands.

"He has honored me of late," he said, "and I have won golden opinions from all sorts of people – which should be worn now in their newest gloss, not cast aside so soon."

Lady Macbeth said nothing, at first. She glared at him – even looking down at the flagon, he could feel the heat of her glower. She turned as though to leave, but then spun back upon her heel, and her words hissed at him as much with bitterness as any desire to go unheard.

"Was the hope *drunk*," she demanded, "wherein you dressed yourself? Has it slept since? And now it wakes, to look so sickly and pale at what it did so freely aspire?" She spat upon the floor – a crass action which shocked him, coming from her. "From this time forward, such is how I will consider your '*love*.' "

He stood, speechless.

"Are you afraid," she seethed, "to be the same in your action and valor as you are in your desire? Will you *take* that crown for which you so lust ... or live a *coward* in your own esteem, letting 'I dare not' follow upon 'I want,' – like the poor cat in the adage, who wanted the fish but would not wet her feet?"

"Prithee, peace!" he snapped, barely remembering to whisper the words. "I dare do *all* that may become a man. He who dares do more is no man at all!"

"What *beast* was it, then," she returned, "that made you break this enterprise to me? When you dared do it, *then* you were a man!" Some of the heat drained from her voice then, and she stepped closer to him. "And, to be more than what you were, you would be so much *more* the man. Neither the time nor place were then suitable, and yet you wanted to make both." She gestured back toward the sounds of the laughing dinner party. "Now they have made themselves, and that fitness of time and place does unmake you!"

Again she turned as though to leave, but this time she held her ground from the onset, her back to him. Macbeth wanted to take her into his arms, but he knew that her emotions – and his own, in honesty – stormed in far too much turmoil.

In a low voice, which he could barely hear, she whispered, "I have suckled a child, and know how tender it is to love the babe that milks me ..."

More than anything she had spoken thus far, this astonished Macbeth. He knew that she had wedded before, that she had borne a child, only to lose both husband and child to the savagery of their time; all of which happened before they had ever laid eyes upon one another. And to his memory, she had never before spoken of her child in his presence.

And then, to his further astonishment, she continued, "... yet I would, while it was smiling in my face, have plucked my nipple from his boneless gums, and dashed the brains out, had *I* so sworn to do as *you* have sworn to do this."

She turned back to him, tears evident in her eyes. He knew she meant it, every word.

How could he stand weak before such strength?

"If we should fail?" he asked.

She smiled and shook her head, reaching up to caress his cheek. "We 'fail'? Only screw your courage to the sticking-place of your crossbow, and we'll *not* fail." She flicked her eyes toward the dining chamber, but a raucous wave of laughter assured they were in no danger of being overheard. Still, she could not help but lower her whisper as she continued, "When Duncan is asleep – to which his day's hard journey shall soundly invite him – I will so overpower his two chamberlains with wine and revelry that their memory, the warden of the brain, shall be a fume, and the receptacle of reason only the limbeck of a distillery."

When Macbeth nodded, his eyes glossing in consideration, she leaned closer still, her lips near his ear.

"When their drenched natures lie in swinish sleep, as in a death ... what *cannot* you and I perform upon the unguarded Duncan? What could we *not* put upon his drunken officers – who shall bear the guilt of our great act?"

Macbeth continued to stare off into space for several long seconds more. But just when Lady Macbeth began to think that she had pushed him too far, that she had lost the cause, he finally beamed down at her, and his feverish eyes glistened in the shadows, radiating the excitement of ambition – and of heated lust.

"Bring forth men-children only!" he fairly growled, his hands wandering her form in areas usually reserved for the bedchamber. "For your undaunted spirit should compose nothing *but* males."

He kissed her, fiercely. For an instant she thought he might not stop there, so intense was his passion, but then he pulled away to speak further while his hands continued to roam.

"Will it not be believed, when we have marked with blood those sleepy two of his own chamber – and used their very daggers – that *they* have done it?"

"Who dares believe it otherwise," she returned, swept along by his fervor – which was, in truth, inflaming an ardor of her own, "as we shall make our griefs and clamor roar upon his death?"

Once more, she thought he might actually lift her into his arms and carry her somewhere more private ... until he stepped away, calming himself on multiple levels. But his eyes remained as febrile as ever.

"I am settled," Macbeth stated, and she did not doubt it, "and shall strain my entire body to this terrible feat." He offered Lady Macbeth his arm, prepared to escort his wife back to the dining chamber, back to Duncan. "Away, and mock the world with fairest show: False face must hide what the false heart doth know."

PART TWO

CHAPTER ONE

Late that night, Banquo, feeling out of sorts, wandered into the inner courtyard of Macbeth's castle. His feet shuffled, his shoulders sagged, and yet he ambled onward. Most of the torches were out now, so he took one from the wall to light his way, as the stars above seemed particularly distant to his unsettled eyes.

He had not traveled far before he spied a lone figure near the far end of the courtyard. It struck him with both amazement and amusement that restlessness might be shared by kin.

"How goes the night, boy?" he asked of Fleance, his son.

The boy jolted, nearly crying out before realizing it was his father who had spoken. Banquo noted that the lad had been admiring one of the great swords Macbeth used to decorate the courtyard walls.

"The moon is down;" Fleance replied with a slight stammer, still recovering, "I have not heard the clock."

Banquo grunted. "And the moon goes down at twelve."

Fleance considered the gloomy sky. "I take it, it is later, sir." The boy glanced once more at the decorative sword, then swallowed a sigh as he prepared to follow his father.

Banquo smiled. "Hold ..."

Fleance looked up, waiting.

Drawing his own weapon from its sheath, he inverted his grip and offered the hilt to his son. "Take my sword."

Fleance's face lit up to outshine the torchlight. Before this, Banquo had limited him to his beaten practice blade during his swordsmanship lessons. He bowed his young head at this surprising honor, and took the heavy sword from his father's grasp.

Banquo watched Fleance weigh the weapon, then considered the night sky once more. "There's economy in heaven," he gestured toward the dim stars, "their candles are all out."

Fleance nodded his agreement, and Banquo noticed for the first time that his son was shivering a bit; the silly boy had taken his nighttime stroll without bringing along a proper cloak.

Chuckling, Banquo removed his own cloak and draped it over his son's shoulders. "You take that, too."

Fleance bowed his double-thanks now, and took a few steps forward before giving the sword a few tentative swings.

Banquo smiled, but the warmth soon drained away. *A heavy weariness lies like lead upon me ... and yet I dread to sleep. Merciful powers, restrain in me the cursed thoughts that nature gives way to when I rest!*

Movement to his right drew Banquo out of his bleak contemplation. Two additional figures approached, the one in the rearmost carrying the torch, leaving the nearer individual's features lost in shadow. It was very likely one of his fellow noblemen, but then, they had just quelled yet another rebellion ...

"Give me my sword," he ordered Fleance. His son

looked at him, followed his gaze toward the advancing men, and hurried to pass over the blade. Banquo then called out, "Who's there?"

"A friend," came Macbeth's voice.

Banquo stood down. "What, sir, not yet at rest? The King's a-bed." Macbeth reached them, his torch-bearing servant halting a few yards away. "He has been in an unusually pleasant spirit, and sent forth great gifts to your household staff." This reminded Banquo of one such largess he was to have passed along earlier, but Macbeth had been absent from the dining chamber at the time. "He greets your wife with this diamond, by the name of 'most kind hostess,' and concluded in measureless content." He produced the diamond from an inner pocket and presented it to Macbeth.

Macbeth accepted the gift with a bow of his head. "Being unprepared for his visit, our will to serve became the servant to *defective* entertainment, which otherwise should have worked without limit."

Banquo dismissed this with a grunt. "All's well."

On an unspoken command by the master of the castle, all four set out to return to the main tower; the servant, of course, brought up the rear as the party moved on.

Banquo lowered his voice and commented to Macbeth, "I dreamt last night of the three Weïrd Sisters." When Macbeth did not immediately respond, he added, "To you, they have showed some truth—"

"I think not of them," Macbeth remarked, which seemed to close the subject. But a moment later, he continued, "Yet, when we can coax an hour to serve, we would spend it in some words upon that business." He looked to Banquo. "If you would grant the time."

"At your kindest leisure," Banquo assured him.

They had reached the tower now, with Banquo and Fleance's sleeping arrangements up the stairway to the left. Before they went their separate ways, however, Macbeth caught Banquo slightly off-guard with his next, soft-spoken words.

"If you shall support my cause, when it is time ... it shall make honor for you."

Banquo looked into Macbeth's eyes, but whatever machinations might have been at work behind them were well hidden. Cautiously, he said, "So long as I lose no honor in seeking to augment it, but still keep my bosom free of blame and allegiance unblemished ... I shall be willing to hear."

Macbeth stared back at him, a slight smile haunting his lips; Fleance shuffled, uneasy with this odd exchange between his father and the great General.

At last, Macbeth's smile widened, growing more amiable, as he gestured up the stairway before them. "Good rest in the meanwhile!"

Banquo nodded, and gave his son a light push up the stairs. "Thanks, sir. The same to you."

Macbeth stared after them until they climbed out of sight, then turned to his servant.

"Go bid your mistress," he commanded, "when my drink is ready, she shall strike upon the bell. Then get to bed."

The servant nodded, bowed, placed the torch into a nearby sconce, then hastened up the stairway to the right, which led to the bedchamber of his master and mistress ... and, further on, the guest quarters of King Duncan.

Macbeth followed the servant with his eyes, and when the young man was gone from sight, he turned his gaze to the diamond still resting in his palm. It was an impressive stone, to be sure; not one worthy of a King's crown, perhaps, but close. As the evening's festivity carried forth, Duncan had grown so inebriated, he had probably forgotten all about passing the diamond along; leave it to honest Banquo not to simply keep the precious stone for himself. He held the clear gem up to eye level, watching it sparkle even in the sparse torchlight. Twinkling, glistening ...

Something else was glistening now, just beyond his focus. He shifted his eyes ...

The diamond fell from Macbeth's numb fingers, forgotten. He gasped as he marveled at the ghostly blade hovering in front of him.

Is this a dagger which I see before me, the handle toward my hand? Come, let me clutch thee.

Macbeth reached out, his pulse quickening at the thought of wielding such a bright, jeweled, fantastic dirk of perfection ...!

And yet, his hand passed right through the beautifully crafted hilt. He tried again, with no greater results.

I have thee not, and yet I see thee still. Are you not, fatal vision, sensible to feeling *as well as to sight?* He lowered his hand. *Or are you but a dagger of the* mind, *a false creation, proceeding from my feverish brain?*

He took a small step forward, drawing his own blade from its sheath at the back of his belt. Oh, but how his paled in comparison to the beauty before him!

I see you yet, in form as palpable as this which now I draw.

He took a second step forward, then hesitated as the phantom withdrew from him, drifting toward the stairway to the right. He smiled at this.

You lead me the way that I was going – and such an instrument I was to use. My eyes are made the fools of the other senses, or else worth more than all the rest!

He blinked as he took yet another step forward, following the dagger ... then stopped short when he realized that the phantom was no longer glistening in quite the same way. Before, its silvery blade prompted the bright display; now, it shined with a dark, red liquid he knew all too well.

I see you still; and on your blade and hilt are splashes of blood, *which was not so before.* He shook his head, suddenly annoyed with himself, and dismissed the apparition, whispering aloud, "There's no such thing."

And sure enough, the phantom blade faded from sight.

Macbeth sighed, nodding. *It is the bloody business which invents thus to my eyes. Now, over half the world, nature seems dead, and wicked dreams abuse their curtained sleep; witchcraft celebrates their pale goddess Hecate with offerings; and age-withered Murder, aroused by his sentinel, the wolf – whose howl is his watchword – thus ... with his stealthy pace, like the Roman King Tarquin's rape of Lucrece ... strides towards his victim, moving like a ghost.*

Macbeth edged toward the staircase, treading carefully as he peered at the ground beneath his feet.

You sure and firm-set earth, hear not my steps, or which way they walk ... for I fear your very stones betray my whereabouts, and take the heavy silence from this moment – which now suits it.

He hesitated at the bottom of the stairs, his feet somehow unwilling to take the first step. His self-vexation grew further as he whispered, "And while I *threat*, Duncan still lives." He shook his head again, hard. "Words to the *heat* of deeds give way to *cold*, weakening breath."

From the tower above, he heard a soft bell chime – his signal from Lady Macbeth that Duncan's chamberlains were incapacitated, that his path was now clear.

So be it.

I go, and it is done; the bell invites me.

Macbeth ascended the stairs.

Hear it not, Duncan, for it is a knell that summons thee to Heaven ... or to Hell.

Chapter Two

Hiding within the shadows of the very same courtyard, Lady Macbeth awaited her husband's triumphant return, her mood so close to giddy that she could barely keep still. She rocked, she swayed, and she drank heavily of the hot milk-and-wine posset which she had shared so very freely with the King's chamberlains. She had also loosened the top of her sleeping gown, preparing for carnal celebration with her King-to-be.

She giggled at her own attitude, given the weight of what was taking place in the tower above.

That which has made them drunk, she thought as she considered her posset, before taking another drink, *has made me* bold; *what has quenched them has given me fire—!*

Her contemplation was interrupted as a shrill cry echoed through the night. This startled her into a sharp "Hark!" But she quickly soothed herself.

Peace! It was the owl that shrieked – like the bellmen the night before an execution, which gives the sternest goodnight.

Lady Macbeth relaxed, slumping back against a water barrel. She reclined onto her elbows, her legs spread a bit further than some would consider "ladylike," as she stared toward the staircase and visualized what her husband was doing at this very moment.

Macbeth is about it now, she thought with a light moan. *The doors are open; and the King's drunken chamberlains do mock their duties with snores – I have drugged their possets, that death and nature do so contend about them, one could not tell whether they live or die.* This last made her giggle again, though even she would have been hard pressed to explain exactly why.

Then, from the stairs above, a voice – Macbeth's? She thought so, but she wasn't certain! – called out, "Who's there? What, ho!"

Lady Macbeth bolted upright. "Alack," she whispered in dismay, "I am afraid they have awaked, and it is not done! The murder attempt, and not the deed, ruins us. Hark!"

She held her breath, straining to detect any sound, the slightest hint of what might be transpiring – the idea of which no longer aroused her. *I laid their daggers ready; he could not miss them!* She recalled the sight of the sleeping King, lying before her. *Had Duncan not resembled my father as he slept,* I *would have done it!*

Then Macbeth appeared before her.

"My husband!" she sighed with relief.

But Macbeth was fraught with tension. "I have done the deed," he stated in a flat tone; then, before she could respond, he demanded, "Did you not hear a noise?"

Addled, she replied, "I heard the owl scream and the crickets cry. Did *you* not speak?"

"When?"

"Now."

"As I descended?"

"Aye."

"Hark!" Macbeth blurted, lurching around as though reacting to some sound; she heard nothing. "Who lies in the second chamber?" he whispered as he pointed up at the tower windows with his left hand.

She thought for a brief moment. "Donalbain."

But Macbeth's gaze had shifted, fixating upon the very hand which he had used to point, at the thick, fresh blood which covered it. He whispered so quietly that his wife could barely hear, "This is a sorry sight ..."

Oh, no. Once he committed to the act, she had hoped that surely his weakness of volition had been banished. "A foolish thought," she told him, forcing a smile of encouragement to her lips, "to say a 'sorry' sight."

Her false jubilation did not move him. In a shaky voice, he continued, "There's one who did laugh in his sleep, and one cried 'Murder!' that they did wake each other; I stood and heard them. But they did say their prayers, and settled again to sleep."

She had to get him off this thread! "There are two lodged together—"

"One cried 'God bless us!' and 'Amen' the other," Macbeth continued unbroken, "as though they had seen me with these grisly hangman's hands. Listening to their fear, I could not say 'Amen,' when they did say 'God bless us!' "

"Consider it not so deeply!" she implored.

"But why could *I* not pronounce 'Amen'?" he begged of her, nearing panic. "I had most need of blessing, and 'Amen' stuck in my throat!"

Taking him by the shoulders – and trying, but failing, to produce another smile of optimism – Lady Macbeth said, "These deeds must *not* be thought upon after these ways; to do so, it will make us mad."

Macbeth shook his head, a wild look in his eyes. "I thought I heard a voice cry, 'Sleep no more! Macbeth does murder sleep' – the *innocent* sleep; sleep that knits up the raveled silken filament of care; the death of each day's life; sore laborer's bath; balm of hurt minds; great nature's main course, chief nourisher in life's feast—"

"What do you mean?" she demanded, baffled and frightened by his rambling.

"Still it cried, 'Sleep no more!' to all the house; 'Glamis has murdered sleep, and therefore Cawdor shall sleep no more – *Macbeth shall sleep no more*'!"

Lady Macbeth placed a trembling hand over his mouth, to silence his woes and hush his voice against discovery. "*Who* was it that thus cried?" she asked, willing him to see that this so-called voice must have been born of his imagination. When his eyes remained glassy and dreadful, she continued, "Why, worthy Thane, you do loosen your noble strength, to think so brain-sickly of things."

He shuddered and shook his head slightly, but at least he remained silent.

She removed her hand from his face and took his shoulders in a gentle embrace. "Go get some water," she whispered, guiding him over to the barrel against which she had so recently reclined, "and wash this filthy evidence from your hand—"

That was when she saw what Macbeth still clasped in his right hand. She, as he, had been so distracted by his focus upon his bloody left, she had not realized ...!

Lady Macbeth gasped, "Why did you bring these *daggers* from the place? They must remain there!" She turned him around and pushed him back toward the staircase. "Go carry them, and smear the sleepy chamberlains with blood."

But Macbeth dug in his heels, shaking his head so fiercely this time that his hair whipped around like a madman's. "I'll go *no more*," he stated with finality, some steel returning to his voice. "I am afraid to *think* of what I have done; I dare not *look* on it again."

"Infirm of purpose!" she snapped, losing her patience in the face of his cowardice. She wanted to slap him, but instead seized the weapons from his clammy hand. "Give *me* the daggers. The sleeping and the dead are like pictures; it is the eye of childhood that fears a painted devil!" She stormed away, speaking more to herself than to her husband as she added, "If Duncan still bleeds, I'll adorn the faces of the chamberlains with it all, for it must seem *their* guilt."

And then Macbeth was alone.

He stared after his wife for a few moments, then down at his bloody hands. She was right, he knew; it was foolish to have brought the murder weapons downstairs with him. But from the moment he sank the blades deep into Duncan's chest – had Duncan awakened at the last moment? He thought so, but could not be sure! – it were as though his body had taken on a will of its own, distinct from his native mind. Stabbing Duncan repeatedly, slashing his throat for good measure, and then trudging down here, into the arms of his "adoring" wife—

A knock resounded from the outer courtyard, and Macbeth very nearly screamed.

"From where is that knocking?" he choked. Then he closed his eyes and drew a deep breath. "How is it with me, when every noise appalls me?" He must regain control of himself!

But when he opened his eyes once more, he wished he hadn't, for their first view was that of his blood-soaked hands.

"Whose hands are here? Ha! They pluck out mine eyes."

Tottering around, he sank his hands elbow-deep into

the water barrel, as his Lady had indicated. The blood quickly began to fade, yes ... and yet, he saw it still.

Will all great Neptune's ocean wash this blood clean from my hand? No, this my hand will rather crimson the multitudes of seas, making the green waters all red.

A footstep from behind brought him whirling about, but he found it was only Lady Macbeth returning. She, too, now bore sanguinary witness from fingertips to forearms, and she held her hands away from her body. Her expression was odd, cold and detached, but with just a hint that she might be close to tears.

Her voice, however, when she spoke, was pure ice. "My hands are of your color; but *I* shame to wear a heart so white."

Husband and wife stared at one another, their eyes locked. And for the briefest moment, Macbeth felt an urge, a strong one, to wrap his tainted hands around her haughty throat—!

The knock he had heard before repeated, startling both of them out of their strange contest of wills.

Lady Macbeth tried to speak, but had to clear her throat first before saying, "I hear a knocking at the south entry." She thought for a second, then continued, "We must retire to our bedchamber."

She rushed forward, plunging her hands into the water barrel, scrubbing them against one another.

"A little water clears us of this deed," she said with pride that he found vexing. A moment later, she held them up for his inspection. "How easy is it, then! *Your* resolve has deserted you." She turned her back on him, heaving herself against the water barrel until it tipped over, spilling its tinged contents to soak into the earth.

The knock returned, evolving to sound a bit more

impatient to Macbeth's ears.

"Hark!" Lady Macbeth noted as well, "more knocking." She stepped closer to him. "Get on your nightgown, lest occasion call us, and show us to be night-watchers." She spun him about and pushed him toward the tower, adding a harsh, "Be not lost so poorly in your thoughts!"

Macbeth allowed her to drive him forward. "To know my deed ... it would be best to *remain* lost in my thoughts."

They had not quite reached the tower entrance when the knocking echoed around them once more. Macbeth gazed up at the window which he knew looked in upon the late King's chambers.

Wake Duncan with your knocking! I wish you could!

Part Two

Chapter Three

The knocking continued, sounding off the outer courtyard walls until, at long last, a begrimed and very drunken porter staggered out of his office. The older man tottered off in the wrong direction until the knock repeated itself once more, bringing him around.

"Here's a knocking indeed!" the inebriated fellow grumbled aloud. He wiped a hand over his bearded face and shook his head, to little avail. "If a man were porter of *Hell-gate*, he would have plenty of turning the key ..."

For reasons that he could not have articulated – as was often the way of men in drink – the gatekeeper found this extremely amusing. He chuckled, then cackled when the knocking returned.

"Knock, knock, knock!" he called back at the south entry, even as he stumbled toward it. He chuckled some more, then put on what he considered an unhallowed voice as he continued, "Who's there, in the name of Beelzebub?" He mimed opening the door, even though it was still some distance from him. "Here's a farmer," he stated in his affected voice, "that hanged himself on the expectation of plentiful grain but lost profits. You've come in time!" He waggled his finger. "Have enough handkerchiefs about you – here you'll sweat for it!"

The knock returned, more insistent than ever. The

porter moved no faster.

"Knock, knock!" he continued his game. "Who's there, in ..." He paused a moment, a confused expression on his face, then shrugged. "... in the other devil's name? Faith, here's a crafty perjurer, that could swear in *both* the scales of justice against *either* scale; who committed enough treason 'for God's sake,' yet could not equivocate his way to Heaven! Oh, come in, equivocator!"

Yet more knocking; the porter kept moving in the general direction of the gate, but took his time in doing so.

"Knock, knock, knock! Who's there? Faith, here's an English tailor come hither, for stealing fabric out of tight French breeches. Come in, tailor; here you may heat your iron!"

He laughed hardest at this jest – imagine, going to Hell for cheating your customers of fabric! – but when the knocking came again, closer on the former round's heels and sharper than ever, the game began to wear thin even for the porter.

"Knock, knock ... never any quiet! Who are you?" At last, some of the alcoholic warmth began to bleed from him, and he trembled. "But this place is too cold for Hell. I'll devil-porter it no further. I had thought to have let in some of *all* professions that go the primrose way to the everlasting bonfire of Hell."

He was very close to the entryway now, and felt the pounding on his own head as the gate shuddered under the latest knocking.

"Right away, right away!" he snapped. Then, vying for a tip as he unlocked the gate, he added, "I pray you, remember the porter."

The gate opened upon two well-dressed, and very

irritated, Scottish noblemen. The porter, drunk though he was, attempted to stand a bit taller, as he recognized them both: Lennox, who stood with his fist poised to knock further, and the Thane of Fife, Macduff.

"Was it so late, friend," came Macduff's clipped words, "when you went to bed, that you do lie so late now?"

The porter blinked in confusion and repressed indignation. The sun had not yet fully arisen; how could the Thane accuse him of lying "late"? But the man knew his station and, rather than defend his honor, he opted to answer the nobleman with levity in mind. "In faith, sir, we were carousing till the second cock of three in the morning; and drink, sir, is a great provoker of three things..."

When the porter did not continue, Macduff sighed and asked, "What three things does drink especially provoke?"

"Indeed, sir," the porter replied as he pointed at his reddened nose, "nose-painting, sleep, and urine. Lechery, sir, it provokes ... and unprovokes." He lifted his right hand and held his forefinger erect. "It provokes the desire, but ..." He then let his finger fall flaccid. "... it takes away the performance."

In spite of their pique, Macduff and Lennox exchanged an amused, and knowing, glance.

"Therefore," the porter continued, pleased with himself, "much drink may be said to be an *equivocator* with lechery:" The man giggled at the word "equivocator," for reasons neither nobleman understood. "It makes him, and it mars him; it sets him on, and it takes him off; it persuades him, and disheartens him; makes him stand to ..." He winked at the men. "... and *not* stand to!" He cackled now. "In conclusion, it deceives him in an erotic dream, and, giving him the lie, leaves him with urine." The porter then took a clumsy bow.

Macduff chuckled, though it was marked with a touch of disdain. "I believe drink gave *you* 'the lie' last night."

The porter shrugged and nodded. "That it did, sir, in the very throat on me; but I repaid him for his lie ..." The man shuffled around in an awkward pantomime, as though he were wrestling with an embodied enemy. "...and, I think, being too strong for him – though he unsteadied my legs sometimes! – yet I managed to cast him out." And with that, the porter mimed vomiting all over the ground.

Having had enough of the show, Macduff asked, "Is your master stirring?"

The porter again considered the early hour, and pondered the best phrasing to say "Of course not!" to a Thane. But then he was relieved of his dilemma when his master, Macbeth, emerged from the gateway between the inner and outer courtyards; he still wore his nightgown but had very clearly stirred, indeed.

Macduff spied him as well. "Our knocking has awaked him," he said to Lennox – though he made sure to meet the tardy porter's eye as well, "here he comes."

"Good morrow, noble sir," Lennox called as Macbeth crossed the yard toward them.

"Good morrow, both," Macbeth called back.

As they moved to meet him in the middle, Macduff asked, "Is the King stirring, worthy Thane?"

Suffering from no such class conflict as his porter – who had quietly staggered away – Macbeth looked pointedly up to the barely-pink dawn sky. "Not yet."

Macduff acknowledged the hour with a nod as they

came together, and he shook Macbeth's hand. "Duncan did command me to call early on him. I have almost missed the hour."

Macbeth nodded his own recognition – after all, when the King commands, what is a mere Thane to do? He then indicated that Macduff and Lennox should follow him back the way he had come. "I'll bring you to him."

As they passed through one courtyard to another, Macduff peered about himself. He spied only one servant, yawning as he attempted to clean up after a water barrel that had apparently tipped over in the night. Given Macbeth's status, he would have expected to see far more than a single servant and drunken porter; the previous night's festivities must have been immoderate indeed. He was not certain if he should feel relief or disappointment that he and Lennox had been called away by duty when the evening had been young.

As they entered the far tower and ascended the right-hand staircase, Macduff commented to Macbeth, "I know this hosting is a joyful trouble to you, but yet it *is* trouble."

They reached the second landing, down which Macbeth proceeded as he shrugged and smiled. "The labor we *delight* in cures pain."

Truly spoken, as Macduff noted that the Thane of Cawdor displayed no personal symptoms of a raucous night; in fact, Macbeth appeared quite serene.

As they reached the end of the corridor, Macbeth stopped and gestured as he announced, "This is the door."

Macduff nodded – while Macbeth might suffer no aftereffects of their carousal, Duncan might not be so lucky. Who desired to awaken a cantankerous King? "I'll make so bold to call," he told them, "for it is my appointed service."

Macbeth and Lennox both chuckled – better he than they! Macduff sighed a bit theatrically, then entered the bedchamber.

Lennox turned to Macbeth. "The King goes hence today?"

"He does," Macbeth confirmed, "he did appoint so."

Lennox nodded, then commented in a grave tone, "The night has been unruly. Where we slept, our chimneys were blown down, and, so they say, lamenting moans were heard in the air – strange screams of *death*, and, with terrible accents, prophesying of dire turmoil and confused events newly hatching to a woeful time. The obscure bird of darkness, the owl, clamored all the livelong night. And some say the earth was feverous and did shake."

Macbeth, whose eyes had widened slightly at Lennox's portends, marveled, "It was a rough night."

Lennox agreed, "My young remembrance cannot parallel an equal to it."

Then the door opened to Duncan's chamber, and Lennox stood erect, expecting the King to appear ...

He did not. Instead, they found themselves staring at a shocked Macduff, whose face shone so pale he appeared almost luminous in the torchlight.

"Oh, horror, horror, *horror*!" Macduff cried, his strangled voice rasping as he spoke. "Tongue nor heart cannot conceive nor *name* you, horror!"

His two witnesses stepped forward, Macbeth a heartbeat quicker than Lennox. "What's the matter?!" they exclaimed together.

"Ruination has now made his masterpiece!" He covered his face with shaking hands, his fingers gripping at the hair upon his forehead. "A most sacrilegious *murder* has broke open the Lord's anointed temple, and stole from it the life of the building!"

Macbeth and Lennox exchanged a confused look. Something terrible had clearly happened, but Macduff was not making sense.

"What is it you say?" Macbeth demanded. " 'The life'?"

Then Lennox felt a chill rush down his spine and curl into his gut. "You mean *His Majesty*?"

Macduff pointed behind him. "Approach the chamber, and destroy your sight with a new Medusa-like Gorgon." He then closed his eyes and shook his head, almost frantic. "Do not bid me speak – *see*, and then speak for yourselves."

Macbeth and Lennox's gazes met once more, then they bolted into Duncan's bedchamber.

Macduff, for his part, opened his eyes so that he could bolt back down the corridor. Foregoing the staircase, he headed for the nearest window, throwing himself toward the gap with such force that he almost tumbled out.

"Awake, *awake*!" he cried out into the inner courtyard. "Ring the alarm-bell! Murder and treason!" He turned in every direction so that those inside the tower and all around might hear him as well. "Banquo and Donalbain! Malcolm! *Awake!* Shake off this downy sleep, the counterfeit death, and look on true death itself! Up, up, and see the great image of *doomsday*!" He wailed with such force, his throat ached. "Malcolm! Banquo! Rise up as from your graves, and walk like spirits, to face this horror! Ring the bell!"

Somewhere, one of Macbeth's servants had clearly awakened and been listening, for the tower bell rang loudly and did not stop.

Macduff slumped beside the window, trying to get his breath back. He heard movement on the landing and thought it would be Lennox and Macbeth, returning from the ghastly sight ...

But it was Lady Macbeth who approached him, her nightgown flowing behind her. Her countenance bore the signature of equal parts concern, bewilderment, and irritation.

"What's the business," she demanded, as strongly as a noblewoman might insist upon a nobleman, "that such a hideous trumpet summons forth the sleepers of the house?" When he did not immediately answer, she implored, "Speak, *speak*!"

Macduff, stymied by reluctance, forced himself to face her. "Oh gentle Lady, it is not for you to hear what I can speak." He dropped his gaze, unable to meet her eye. "The repetition, in a woman's ear, would murder her as it fell."

Lady Macbeth, unquestionably confounded, approached him, opening her mouth to again urge him to speak. Mercifully, Banquo emerged from the staircase at that moment, sparing Macduff the necessity of dispensing the horrible news directly to the Lady of the house.

"Oh, Banquo," Macduff cried to his fellow nobleman, "Banquo, our royal master's murdered!"

Both Banquo and Lady Macbeth stopped in their tracks, stunned. Her hands at her face, Lady Macbeth gasped, "Woe, alas! What, in *our* house?"

"Too cruel anywhere," Banquo moaned. "Dear Duff, I pray you, contradict yourself, and say it is not so."

Again Macduff was granted a reprieve, as all eyes turned when Macbeth and Lennox returned from down the corridor, even as Ross rushed up the stairs to join them.

His head low, and in a voice that indicated a heavy heart, Macbeth proclaimed, "Had I but died an hour before this chance ... I had lived a blessed time; for, from this instant, there's nothing worthwhile in this mortal life – all is nothing but *trivial*." He shook his head, and released a thick sigh. "His renowned Grace is dead; the wine of life is drawn, and all that is left in this wine vault of the world to brag of is the mere *sediment*."

They all remained silent at that; Lennox nodded his agreement, while Ross' jaw sagged in shock as he absorbed the news. Several long seconds later, the King's sons appeared on the scene, only to look around in confusion at the dour gathering.

"What is amiss?" Donalbain asked.

Macbeth stared at the two men for a moment, a dark and thoughtful expression upon his face. At last, he answered, "*You* are, and do not know it. The spring, the head, the fountain of your blood is stopped; the very *source* of it is stopped."

When Malcolm and Donalbain merely looked at one another, befuddled – or, perhaps, in denial – Macduff stated clearly, "Your royal father's murdered."

Donalbain reacted as though Macduff had struck him in the gut, so it was Malcolm who beseeched "Oh, by *whom*?"

Macbeth remained silent, still staring at them, so Lennox answered, "Those of his chamber – as it seemed – had done it. Their hands and faces were all marked with blood; so were their daggers, which we found unwiped upon their pillows. They stared, and were distracted." His face twisted in disgust. "No man's life was to be trusted with them."

Macbeth spoke again, his words now tainted with regret. "Oh, yet I do repent me of my fury ... that I did *kill* them."

Macduff's gaze snapped toward Macbeth, his eyes sharp. "Why did you so?"

Macbeth returned his own sharp glare, even as he realized that *all* eyes were now upon him – and that Lennox, unspeaking witness to his act, took a small step away from him. With indignation, he demanded, "*Who* can be wise, amazed, temperate and furious, loyal and neutral – all in a moment? *No* man! The haste of my violent love for Duncan outran the pauser, *reason*." He gestured, with flourish, to his left. "Here lay Duncan, his silver skin laced with his golden blood; and his gashed stabs looked like a breach in Nature's defenses for *Ruin's* destructive entrance." He gestured to his right. "There, the *murderers*, steeped in the bloody color of their trade, their daggers unmannerly covered with gore!" Macbeth cast about, meeting each of their eyes as he declared, "*Who* could refrain, that had a heart to love Duncan, and in that heart the courage to make his love *known*?"

A bold proclamation it was, the words undeniable. And yet the group – particularly Macduff and Banquo – still scrutinized Macbeth ...

Lady Macbeth suddenly swooned, collapsing against the outer wall, dangerously close to the window through which Macduff himself had nearly fallen in his rush, minutes earlier. "Help me hence," she cried in a stupor, an arm flung across her face, "ho!"

"Look to the Lady," Macduff announced to no one in particular, and thus all the noblemen rushed to her aid.

All save the King's sons.

Making certain that none of the others were currently watching them, Malcolm whispered to

Donalbain, "Why do we hold our tongues, that others may claim this matter as their own?"

"What should be spoken here," Donalbain whispered back, "where our fate, hid in the smallest snake-hole, may rush and *seize* us?" He swallowed, hard. "Let us away; our tears are not yet brewed for weeping."

Malcolm agreed, in a voice that nevertheless shook with emotion, "Nor our strong sorrow prepared for action."

Lady Macbeth appeared to be in full shock now, no longer able to keep her footing; were it not for the surrounding, helping hands, she would have collapsed all the way to the floor.

Attendants for many of the noblemen had arrived, tardy but timely, as Banquo echoed Macduff's words, "Look to the Lady."

The attendants, aware of their sluggish responses to duty – more than one were still a bit intoxicated, while the majority suffered from having been so – hurried to carry the Lady back to her chambers.

Banquo then regarded the group once more. "And when we have our naked frailties hid," he gestured to his own nightgown, and those worn by all but Macduff and Lennox, "that suffer in cold exposure ... let us meet, and question this most bloody piece of work, to know it further." All the men nodded their agreement. Banquo grunted, and continued, "Fears and suspicions shake us. I stand in the great hand of God, and therefore I fight against the secret design of *treasonous malice*."

"And so do *I*," Macduff stated, boldly and without hesitation.

In short order, all the remaining noblemen followed with, "So all." This was followed by an awkward moment of silence – where to go from here? Lady

Macbeth was not the only Scot in shock this morning.

Macbeth filled that silence, emulating Banquo's gesture at the many nightgowns. "Let's quickly put on manly clothing, and meet in the hall together."

"Well contented," the group agreed, and dispersed toward their different bedchambers. Macduff and Lennox descended the stairs, conversing among themselves as Macduff questioned his companion for further details of Macbeth's slaying of Duncan's chamberlains ...

... leaving only Malcolm and Donalbain alone on the landing.

"What will you do?" Malcolm asked his brother.

Donalbain shook his head, at a loss. Banquo had already stated his "suspicions" about this "secret design." How long would it take them to realize who stood to gain the most from Duncan's murder? Especially with Malcolm so recently named the Prince of Cumberland?

"Let's not consort with them," Malcolm decided. "To show an unfelt sorrow is an office which the *false* man does easy." He thought a brief moment – where to seek safe asylum? Not within Scotland! – then added, "I'll go to England."

Donalbain nodded. "To Ireland, I – our separated fortune shall keep us both the safer." He looked out the window and about Macbeth's castle as it loomed around them. "Where we are, there's daggers in men's smiles – the nearer in blood, the nearer bloody."

Malcolm knew Donalbain spoke truly. Here, now, they were in greater danger from their fellow noblemen than they had been from the recent insurgents. Had Macbeth not already slain the apparent assassins in a self-proclaimed rage of righteousness?

Malcolm touched his brother's shoulder. "This murderous shaft that's shot has not yet lighted upon us, and our safest way is to avoid the aim." Donalbain gripped his hand, and nodded once more. "Therefore, to horse, and let us not be particular about leave-taking, but quietly escape. There's justification in that theft, which steals itself away when there's no mercy left."

PART TWO

CHAPTER FOUR

Mere hours later, Ross waited outside Macbeth's castle. Word had spread of Duncan's assassination, and Ross had volunteered to go forth and reassure the people of Inverness that Scotland remained well in hand. He sought to quell fears – both theirs, and his own – of a new insurgency, of further war. When he returned, he felt it best to hold silent vigil outside, to keep his own peace out here in the dreary morning – the earlier pink of dawn was the brightest this day had gotten – rather than interrupt the proceedings underway. After all, what could he add that Macduff, Lennox, or Macbeth could not?

As time crawled by, an old man – whom Ross had seen before, but whose name he could not recall at present – meandered over next to him. Ross nodded in greeting, and the two remained reticent for a time, standing together in the gloom.

At length, the old man commented, "Threescore and ten years I can remember well, within the volume of which time I have seen hours dreadful and things strange..." He shook his head in sadness. "... but this grievous night has made trifles of all former knowings."

Ross sighed, gazing up at the sky, with its dark, heavy clouds. "Ha! – good father, you see the heavens, just as troubled with man's act, threaten this bloody stage.

By the clock, it is day ... and yet dark night strangles the traveling sun." He, too, shook his head. "Is it night's predominance, or the day's *shame*, that darkness does entomb the face of earth, when living light should kiss it?"

"It is unnatural," the old man stated, "even like the deed that's done." He then added quietly, almost embarrassed to share an "omen" with a nobleman, "On last Tuesday, a falcon – circling upward to her highest place in the sky – was hawked at and killed by a *mousing* owl."

Ross picked up the thread of bizarre signs. "Another thing most strange and certain: Duncan's horses – beauteous and swift, the finest of their race – turned wild in nature, broke their stalls, flung out, contending against obedience, as though they would make war with mankind."

The old man nodded; he had heard the dark tale. "It is said they *ate* each other."

"They did so," Ross confirmed, "to the amazement of mine eyes that looked upon it."

Silence fell over the two once more, and only a little more time passed before the castle's south gate opened.

Ross eased a bit when he saw who emerged. "Here comes the good Macduff." He then called to the approaching Thane of Fife, "How goes the world, sir, now?"

Macduff chuckled, but it was a humorless sound. He gave the dark sky a meaningful look. "Why, see you not?"

Ignoring that, Ross asked, "Is it known who did this more than bloody deed?"

Macduff shrugged one shoulder – a subtle gesture which Ross almost missed, yet also spoke volumes as he answered with the faintest hint of rebuke. "Those that

Macbeth has slain."

"Alas, the day!" Ross blurted with a shake of his head. "What good could they intend?"

Again, Macduff shrugged one shoulder. "They were bribed. Malcolm and Donalbain, the King's two sons, are stolen away and fled, which puts upon *them* suspicion of the deed."

Ross flung his arms in loathing. "Against nature still! Thriftless ambition, that will so ravenously devour your own life's means!" He held on to his contempt a moment longer, before deflating under the weight of it all. "Then it is most likely the sovereignty will fall upon Macbeth."

Macduff averted his eyes, staring about the landscape, as he stated, "He is already named, and gone to Scone to be crowned."

Ross wondered at this. Not that Macbeth should be coronated at Scone – it was the ancient capital, and the traditional site for such events – but the swiftness of it all left a bitter taste in his mouth. True, Macbeth was Duncan's cousin, and a respected General, admired by all loyal Scots ... and yet, the impulsive slaying of the accused, before they could be questioned ...

He asked Macduff, "Where is Duncan's body?"

"Carried to Colmekill, the sacred storehouse of his predecessors, and guardian of their bones."

"Will you go to Scone?"

Macduff stared out at the panorama a moment longer, then looked Ross pointedly in the eyes as he said, "No, cousin, I'll to Fife."

Ross considered this. A rejection of Macbeth's claim? An avoidance of swearing his oath of allegiance?

Or simply a man who wished to return to his home and family?

Unsure of what position to take himself, Ross merely said, "Well, I will follow to Scone."

Macduff nodded his understanding, in more ways than one. "Well, may you see things well done there. Adieu!" They shook hands. "Lest our old robes sit easier than our new!"

Ross shuddered. Could things get any worse? Rather than respond to that, he turned to the old man – who had retreated a few feet away as the noblemen spoke. "Farewell, father."

The old man bowed to both of them. "God's blessing go with you, and with those that would make good of bad, and friends of foes!"

All three men turned away, their backs to the castle at Inverness, and departed.

Part Three

Chapter One

The sun shone upon the King's palace at Forres ... and yet, to Banquo, it felt as though the gloom that followed Duncan's murder still hung heavy indeed.

Here again, Banquo found himself in the courtyard of the royal palace of Scotland, but this time he stood alongside his worthy steed, rather than in the company of his fellow soldier and comrade, Macbeth. No, this time that former friend was already deep within those imperial walls, sitting upon the throne.

And Banquo grappled with mixed feelings about this strange twist of events.

You have it now, he thought to his friend. *King, Cawdor, Glamis,* all, *as the weïrd women promised ... and I fear you played most foully for it. Yet it was said it should not stand with your descendants, but that* myself *should be the root and father of many Kings to come.*

Banquo shuddered, a mixture of revulsion and excitement that itself repelled him. Aloud, he whispered, "If there comes truth from them – as upon you, Macbeth, their speeches shine – why, by the truths made good on *you* ... may they not be *my* oracles as well, and set me up in hope?"

A flourishing trumpet call blasted through the air, startling him in guilt against his will. His horse detected

Banquo's stress, and shuffled about more in response to his master's tension than the blaring of the wind instruments; Banquo stroked his mane to soothe him. The regal party had emerged from the primary tower, and approached.

But hush, he chastised himself. *No more.*

The company consisted of King Macbeth and his Queen, of course, as well as Lennox, Ross, and other assorted Lords and Ladies, and their many attendants. Macbeth was conversing with Lennox, while Lady Macbeth appeared to merely bask in the fawning of those around her; the royal pair were clothed in notable finery, with flair beyond what Duncan had ever embraced. When Macbeth spied Banquo, however, he touched his wife's elbow, and together they approached him.

"Here's our chief guest," Macbeth said, ostensibly to his wife but loud enough to be heard by all.

Lady Macbeth replied, just as brassy, "If he had been forgotten, it had been as a gap in our great feast, and wholly unbecoming."

Banquo moved forward to meet his monarch, and bowed his head in acceptance of their flowery adulation.

In a somewhat more intimate tone, the new King then said to him, "Tonight we hold a formal supper, sir, and I'll request your presence."

"Let Your Highness command upon me," Banquo replied, "to which command my duties are, with a most indissoluble tie, forever knit."

Macbeth smiled, then glanced over Banquo's shoulder to his familiar steed. "Ride you this afternoon?"

"Aye, my good Lord."

"I should have else desired your good advice – which has ever been both grave and prosperous – in this day's council; but I'll take it tomorrow." He gestured toward the horse. "Is it far you ride?"

Banquo shrugged with a grunt. "As far, my Lord, as will fill up the time between now and supper – unless]my horse goes faster than expected ..." He mused. "... I must become a borrower of the night for a dark hour or two."

"Don't fail our feast," Macbeth scolded with a smile.

"My Lord, I will not."

Macbeth then stepped in closer, and dropped his voice lower still; it was a familiar sharing of confidence, and for a moment, Banquo felt as though his old friend were back. "I hear my bloody cousins," Macbeth told him, speaking of Malcolm and Donalbain, "are bestowed in England and in Ireland – not confessing their cruel parricide, but filling their hearers with *strange* invention." He paused, staring at Banquo's face with great intent, as though searching for something.

Banquo stared back at his friend-cum-King, his expression betraying nothing.

Macbeth's demeanor brightened once more as he concluded, "But more of that tomorrow, when together we shall have stately business concerning us jointly." He clapped Banquo on the shoulder. "Hurry to your horse; adieu, till you return at night."

Banquo bowed to his King and Queen, then retreated to his awaiting steed.

Seconds before he mounted, Macbeth called, "Does Fleance go with you?"

A simple question, delivered in the most casual manner ... and yet, something about the mention of his son struck a wave of cold deep within Banquo. Forcing a nonchalant grin to grace his lips, he looked back and replied, "Aye, my good Lord. Our time does call upon us."

Macbeth's own placid smile told Banquo nothing as

the King raised his hand. "I wish your horses swift and sure of foot; and so I do commend you to their backs." He waved Banquo on. "Farewell."

Banquo nodded his thanks and, grateful to break eye contact, he leaped upon his horse and hurried out through the palace gates to meet his waiting son ... and tried not to consider dark things for a time.

Behind him, Macbeth turned to face his retinue. He announced, "Let every man be master of his time till seven at night. To make your company the sweeter welcome, I will keep to myself till suppertime ..." He glanced sideways toward his wife, who had taken a step toward his side. "... alone." His followers nodded their understanding; only Lady Macbeth displayed a touch of confusion upon her face, and Macbeth spoke almost directly to her as he concluded, "Until then, God be with you!"

The group began to break apart, each dispersing into directions of their choosing and needs. Lady Macbeth lingered for a heartbeat, then she also walked away.

Before they could stray too far, Macbeth caught the eye of one young lad. "Sirrah," he addressed the boy with the rather contemptuous term, "a word with you."

The attendant hustled back to his King, his eyes low and his shoulders hunched.

Macbeth said nothing at first, merely ambled his way toward the nearest servants' quarters.

The boy followed, dreading what might come. Had he done something to warrant a beating? Or did the King entertain certain "tastes" of which he had not been warned?

As he entered the quarters, Macbeth noted a handful of courtyard servants, whom he dismissed with a sharp snap of his fingers. When the quarters were emptied, he addressed the trailing lad, "Do those men wait upon my pleasure?"

For the briefest moment, the boy panicked, not knowing to whom the King was referring. Then he fairly sobbed with relief as he recalled the matter at hand. "They are, my Lord," he breathed, "outside the palace gate."

"Bring them before me."

The boy bowed so long he almost stumbled as he hurried to leave.

Now alone, Macbeth attempted patience, but it defied him. His business, the need having grown in his gut over his brief tenure as King, demanded his focus with increasing ferocity. He reached up and removed his crown, then gazed upon it, measuring its weight – literal and moral – and its allure.

To be thus, Macbeth thought as he studied the symbol of his Kingship, *is nothing, unless I am to be* safely *thus.*

He returned the crown to his head and paced the service quarters.

My fears of Banquo stick deep, and that which must be feared reigns in his natural nobility. It is much that he dares, and, together with that dauntless temper of his mind, he has a wisdom that does guide his valor to act in safety.

His stride lengthened.

There is none but he *whose being I do fear; and, under him, my guardian spirit is* cowed – *as, it is said, Mark Antony's was frightened by Octavius Caesar.*

He paced faster.

Banquo chided the Weïrd Sisters when they first put the name of 'King' upon me, and bade them speak to him; then, prophet-like, they hailed him father to a line of

Kings. Upon my *head they placed a fruitless crown, and put a barren scepter in my grip, from there to be wrenched by another family's hand – no son of* mine *succeeding to the throne!*

He paced faster still.

If it be so, then I have defiled my mind for Banquo's *heirs; for* them *I have murdered the gracious Duncan; only for* them *I have put bitterness in the vessel of my peace, and given my eternal soul to the common enemy of man, the Devil, to make them Kings – the seeds of* Banquo, Kings!

On that, Macbeth abruptly stopped, his hands balled into tight fists.

"Rather than have it so," he whispered through clenched teeth, "come, Fate, into the arena, and fight me to the end!" A shuffling footstep drew his attention to the quarters' entrance. "Who's there?"

The boy attendant returned and bowed low, and he did not enter alone. Behind him trailed two vile men, and Macbeth knew those dirty beasts for what they truly were:

Murderers.

"Now go to the door," he commanded the boy, "and stay there till I call."

The attendant bowed once more, and retreated in haste.

Macbeth stared at the pair in silence for a stretch; this particular setting did not lend itself to his royal power, so he reminded them thus with the weight of his bearing. The smaller, younger criminal looked to the floor within seconds; the older, scarred reprobate took a bit longer, but Macbeth was pleased to see them both cowed before he spoke.

"Was it not yesterday we spoke together?"

The first murderer, the younger one, answered. "It

was, so please Your Highness."

Macbeth grunted – and the similarity to Banquo's tendency was not lost on him. "Well then, now have you considered my speeches?"

The murderers glanced at one another, then back to the floor.

Macbeth continued, "You know that it was *he*, in the times past, who held you so out of fortune – which you thought had been *my* innocent self. This I made good to you in our last conference, reviewed the proof with you – how you were deceived, how thwarted, the instruments used, who worked them, and all things else that might say, even to half a soul and to a mind crazed: 'Thus ... did ... *Banquo*'."

Again, the younger one spoke. "You made it known to us."

"I *did* so," Macbeth returned, sharp enough to make him flinch. Then, in a calmer, relaxed and reasonable voice, he continued, "And went further, which is now the point of this second meeting." He placed his fists on his hips, and looked back and forth between them with an expression of exaggerated disbelief. "Do you find your patience *so* predominant in your nature that you can *let this go*?"

The men shuffled in place, their eyes pointed downcast.

"Are you so gospelled by the forgiveness of Christ," Macbeth hammered, "to *pray* for this 'good' man and for *his* children, whose heavy hand has bowed you to an early grave and beggared *your* children forever?"

Once more, the first spoke; this time with some semblance of dignity. "We are *men*, my liege."

Macbeth rolled his eyes and scoffed as he began to pace around them. "Aye, in the catalogue you go for 'men' – as hounds and greyhounds, mongrels, spaniels, curs, shaggy lap-dogs, long-haired water-dogs, and demi-wolves are all called by the name of 'dogs.' But the list of values *distinguishes* the swift, the slow, the subtle, the watchdog, the hunter – every one according to the gift which bounteous nature has enclosed in him; whereby he does receive particular description in contrast to the file that writes them all haphazardly ..."

At last, Macbeth had made a full circuit around the criminals, and now he stood and faced them full-on.

"... and so it is with *men*. Now, if you have a station in this file, *not* in the worst rank of manhood, say it; and I will put that business deep within you, whose execution takes your enemy off, grapples you close to the heart and love of *myself* – I wear my health but sickly while *he* lives ... which, in his death, would be *perfect*."

For the first time, the second murderer, the one with the scarred face, spoke. "I am one, my liege," he grumbled, and Macbeth noted his less deferential tone of voice, "whom the vile blows and buffets of the world have so incensed that I am reckless with what I do to spite the world."

Emboldened, the first murderer agreed, "And I another, so weary with disasters, pulled about by fortune, that I would stake my life on *any* chance – to mend it ... or be rid of it."

Macbeth smiled. "Both of you know Banquo was your enemy."

Together, they said, "True, my Lord."

Macbeth nodded. "So is he *mine*; and in such bloody enmity, that every minute of his being thrusts against my heart! And though I could, with barefaced power, sweep him from my sight and bid my will justify it ..." He sighed heavily, demonstrating his frustration. "... yet I must not, due to certain friends that are both his and mine, whose loves I may not drop ... but I must *wail* his fall, whom I myself struck down."

Macbeth stepped closer to them, until they were within arm's reach. A potentially dangerous move, to be sure, were his hands – which he clasped behind his back – not so close to the dagger he stored at the rear of his belt.

"And from there it is," the King said, "that I do make love to your assistance, masking the business from the common eye for sundry, weighty reasons."

The scarred man said, "We shall, my Lord, perform what you command us."

"Though our lives—" the younger one began.

Macbeth waved this away as he stepped back. "Your spirits shine through you. Within this hour, at most, I will advise you where to plant yourselves, acquaint you with the precise information of the time, the moment for it." He held up a pointed finger, tipping it toward each of their faces. "For it must be done tonight, and somewhere away from the palace – always remember that I require a *clearness from suspicion*."

Macbeth returned to pacing, his gaze away from the men as he issued his next instruction.

"And with him – to leave no roughness nor botches in the work – Fleance, his son that keeps him company, whose absence is no less material to me than is his father's, must embrace the *same fate* of that dark hour."

He turned back to regard them; he expected they might balk upon learning they must murder a child, but was pleased to see that, though these emotions were surely present, they did not appear great enough to deter these criminals from earning royal favor.

"Decide for yourselves apart," he commanded them,

"I'll come to you shortly."

The two exchanged a glance, then mumbled together, "We are resolved, my Lord."

Macbeth nodded with great acumen. "I'll call upon you straight away. Stay within."

So dismissed, the murderers bowed and retreated from the service quarters.

Alone, Macbeth drew a deep breath, holding it tight before a slow release.

It is concluded. Banquo, your soul's flight – if it is to find Heaven, it must find it out tonight.

In her private chambers, the Queen changed out of her day-wear as she prepared for that evening's dinner. She wore many different royal vestures over the course of each day, a specific fantasy which had crept up the moment she read her husband's letter of the Weïrd Sisters...

... yet, it did not bring her the pleasure she had imagined.

"Is Banquo gone from court?" Lady Macbeth asked her servant as the woman finished fastening her new garment.

"Aye, madam, but returns again tonight."

Lady Macbeth shook her head, irritated at herself. Of course this was the case; she had stood next to her husband as he and Banquo discussed this very thing not two hours ago! Where was her mind lately?

"Say to the King," she told her servant as she moved to the water bowl and began washing her hands. "I would attend his leisure for a few words."

"Madam, I will," the woman said with a bow, then retreated from the room.

Alone, the Queen thoroughly wiped her hands dry, then crossed the room and fingered the beautiful jewels that were now hers to select for the occasion. But her thoughts drifted elsewhere.

Nothing's gained, but all's spent, where our desire is gotten but without content.

Her hands finally closed upon an attractive choker that matched her dinner dress nicely; it seemed appropriate.

It is safer to be that which we destroy than, by destruction, dwell in doubtful joy.

She jumped as the chamber door flew open. Her husband, her King, stood before her, already dressed for dinner and with an increasingly familiar look of discontent upon his features.

"How now, my Lord," she said to Macbeth with forced geniality, "why do you keep alone, making companions of your sorriest fancies – entertaining those thoughts which should indeed have died with them they think on?" She offered a sympathetic smile, and added softly, "Things without any remedy should be without regard: What's *done* is *done*."

Macbeth did not return her smile as he closed the door behind him. "We have slashed the snake, *not* killed it. She'll close the wound and be herself, while our feeble enmity remains in danger of her former venomous tooth." He lingered where he stood a moment, then stepped further into the room, his fists clenching. "But let the frame of all the universe fall apart – both the celestial and terrestrial worlds suffer – before I should eat my meals in fear and sleep in the affliction of these terrible dreams that shake me nightly!"

Lady Macbeth stared at him, uncertain of how to respond. The murder of Duncan had shaken her – when she thought to admit as much to herself – but her husband was, if anything, growing harder and colder than was to her liking.

Macbeth's next words, however, were more vulnerable. "Better to be with the dead," he said, his eyes downcast, "whom we, to gain our peace, have sent *to* peace ... than to lie in restless frenzy on the torture of the mind." He chuckled then, a dark sound. "Duncan is in his grave; after life's fitful fever, *he* sleeps well. Treason has done its worst to him – neither steel nor poison, domestic malice, foreign levy ... *nothing* can touch him further."

Treading carefully, Lady Macbeth eased her way to him, reaching out to place a cautious hand upon his forearm. "Come on, my gentle Lord" she soothed him, "smooth over your rugged looks." She forced another smile, allowing him to see that it took an effort for her to do so. "Be bright and jovial among your guests tonight."

Macbeth returned her effort this time, but much like his chuckle, she found it uncomfortable to witness. "So I shall, love," he told her, "and so, I pray, be *you*."

He reached up to stroke her chin; a soft touch, and yet she had to fight the urge to withdraw. But *why*, damn it? This was her husband!

"Let your kindest remembrance be given to Banquo," he was saying, "present him special honor, both with eye and tongue: We are unsafe for the while, so we must cleanse our honors in these flattering streams, and make our faces masks to our hearts, disguising what they are."

Once more, she tried, "You must leave this alone."

He shook his head with deep finality. "Oh, my mind is full of *scorpions*, dear wife! You know that Banquo, and his son Fleance, live."

"But in them nature's energy is not eternal."

He cocked his head in acknowledgment and, once again, unsettled her. "There's some comfort yet – they are assailable." He straightened his posture and drew his own false smile back into place; but unlike hers, his now appeared convincing enough. "Then you should be merry! Before the bat has flown his cloistered flight, before the scaly-winged beetle, with his drowsy hums, has rung night's yawning bells to black Hecate's summons ... there shall be done a deed of dreadful note."

Lady Macbeth swallowed hard at that, but otherwise struggled to keep her face neutral. She drifted away from him, but did not want to seem aimless, so she moved to the bowl and began washing her hands again. As casually as she could manage, she asked over her shoulder, "What is to be done?"

When he didn't answer, she glanced back to find him staring at her, his visage a complete blank, as though a wall of stone stood between them.

"Be innocent of the knowledge, dearest chuck," Macbeth stated, the term of endearment easing her not at all, "till you applaud the deed."

Unsure of what else to do or say, she nodded vaguely and returned to scrubbing her hands.

"Come, darkest night," she heard her husband saying at the open window, "blindfold the tender eye of merciful day, and with your bloody and invisible hand, cancel and tear to pieces that great bond of Banquo's descendants which keeps me pale! Light thickens, and the crow makes wing to the rook-filled wood; good things of day begin to droop and drowse, while night's black agents to their preys do rouse."

She shuddered as she dried her hands, then trembled again when she saw the darkness in Macbeth's eyes. They stood across from one another for a moment, then he approached her.

"You marvel at my words," he remarked, "but hold yourself still; bad things begun make themselves *stronger* by further ill." He stopped before her, and held out his arm. "So prithee go with me."

She took his arm. What else could she do?

They proceeded down to the gathering for dinner, and she wished she had taken the time to wash her hands once more.

PART THREE

CHAPTER THREE

In the approaching twilight, within the shadows of the park which stood between the stables and the palace at Forres, three black-clothed men entrenched themselves within the trees.

The first two, the very murderers to whom the King had issued his malevolent instructions, moved with familiarity, while the newcomer trailed at their heels. In short order, the first murderer grew nettled by the third's unwanted presence and turned on him, picking up on the whispered conversation which had begun as they left the main path.

"But who did bid you join with us?"

The third man, unmoved by the young man's hostility, enunciated with clarity as though speaking to a small child, or a halfwit, "Macbeth."

Rankled, the younger man reached for the blade at his belt. But his older partner placed a calming hand upon his wrist.

"He needs not our mistrust," the second murderer told him, "since he shares our duties, and what we have to do, to the precise direction."

Still feeling petulant, the young man grumbled at the newcomer, "Then stand with us. The west yet glimmers with some streaks of day; now the belated traveler spurs his horse quickly to gain his timely inn, and the subject of our watch approaches near."

The third man smirked and opened his mouth, probably to deliver a snide remark, but then his face shifted from contempt to strict business. "Hark!" he whispered. "I hear horses."

They all crouched and drew their blades as a voice called out near the stables, a voice which the first two men knew very well.

"Give us a light there, ho!" Banquo addressed one of the stableboys.

"Then it is *he*," the second murderer said with a nod. "The rest that are within the list of expected guests are already in the King's court."

The first cocked his head at the sound of Banquo's horses trotting into the stables. "His horses go about."

The third glanced over his shoulder toward the barely visible torchlight coming from the palace. "Almost a mile," he commented, "but he does usually, so all men do, make it their walk from here to the palace gate."

The second hunched further as he pointed down the path. "A light," he breathed, "a light!"

A torch appeared, and a few moments later they could see that it was carried by Fleance as he walked alongside his father.

"It is he," the third agreed.

The first, forgetting his previous distrust of the newcomer, crept into position. "Stand to it," he told the others.

They did.

Their targets drew nearer. They could see the pair well, the father walking with a causal hand upon the son's shoulder, their voices mere murmurs until the final moments.

As the wind picked up, Banquo faced it full and commented, "It will be rain tonight."

The first murderer could not resist such an apt opening. Leaping from his hiding place, he bellowed, "Let it come down!" as he struck the torch from Fleance's grasp.

The boy cried out and stumbled back, but even as the three murderers set upon Banquo, they failed to take into account that he was a soldier, a General in the Scottish army, and had survived many rounds of hand-to-hand combat.

Despite the sudden darkness, to which the outlaws were adapted but Banquo was not, Banquo drew his dirk in a heartbeat and parried first one, then two of the incoming, larger and longer blades. He kicked, striking one of his assailants in the knee, downing the man; Banquo almost managed to bury his own blade into the man's exposed neck, before having to instead defend himself from another attack.

"Oh, treachery!" Banquo roared, though he had little hope of his voice carrying such a distance to the castle.

And if it did, would he find allies of sufficient loyalty there? He cursed himself for turning a blind eye to his fears and suspicions, for he had little doubt what motives were behind this assault. Damn the Weïrd Sisters, and damn Macbeth!

The three murderers rallied, nearly surrounding Banquo in a wide arc; they would not underestimate him again.

"Fly, good Fleance," he called over his shoulder, "fly, fly, *fly*!" The murderers charged, and he knew that he could not stand before all of them. Accepting this, he added to his fleeing son, "You may *revenge*!"

But he did survive the charge, though it cost him a

slash across his forearm. And a moment later, he realized why:

Only two of the murderers attacked *him* – the third was chasing after his boy!

"Oh, *villain*!" Banquo howled, and acted without thought or hesitation. He reversed his grip on his dirk and hurled the blade. The park was dark and shadowed, but his aim was true enough – he impaled the third man in the thigh, forcing the criminal to break off his pursuit.

The third, Banquo's blade still in his leg, attempted his own ranged attack, but to his less-trained eye and hand, the darkness was too great, and he missed his mark by a considerable distance.

The boy was gone.

The last thing Banquo saw, as the first two murderers stabbed him repeatedly, was Fleance's escape; his own death, which came quickly, seemed more tolerable for that.

When the third hobbled back to his fellow assailants, he found them still jabbing the corpse, over and over. Enraged at their shortsightedness, he seized the younger man by the arm and forced him around. "Who did strike out the light?" he demanded.

The first blinked stupidly. "Was it not the way?"

The third channeled the pain from his thigh into the loathing of his voice as he spat, "There's but *one* down – the *son* is fled."

The second groaned as he jerked his sword from Banquo's steaming back. "We have lost best half of our affair."

The first stewed for a moment, then declared, "Well ... let's away, and say to Macbeth how much *is* done."

The third only glared at him, but the second nodded – what else could they do?

PART THREE

CHAPTER FOUR

The dining hall of the royal palace teemed with food, drink, and staff tending to all. The tables were set according to old tradition – those of higher rank sat nearer the raised, foremost table, that of the King and Queen – and candles and torches lit every nook.

With a flourish, the hall doors were opened, and Macbeth and his Lady entered, followed by Ross, Lennox, and other Lords, and all the attendants thereof; the hall transitioned from preparation to execution in a heartbeat.

"You know your own ranks," Macbeth declared to all, "sit down. Once for all of you, a hearty welcome!"

A brief applause sounded as the many Lords replied, "Thanks to Your Majesty!"

As the noblemen began seating themselves, Macbeth ambled along the guests' tables. "I will mingle with society and play the humble host." A smattering of laughter returned as he filled a random Lord's cup with wine, then he continued with a gesture toward his wife, "Our hostess keeps her chair of state, but in best time we will request her welcome."

Lady Macbeth replied with a raised goblet, "Pronounce it for me, sir, to all our friends, for my heart speaks – they are welcome."

More polite clapping and murmured responses, but

Macbeth only heard those in passing; his focus lay upon a discrete door at the far end of the dining hall, which had opened to expose, briefly, the face of the younger murderer.

With smooth recovery, he said to his Queen, "See, they respond to you with their hearts' thanks!" He made a show of evaluating the guests' tables, then indicated an open seat. "Both sides are even; here I'll sit in the midst." He began backing toward the unobtrusive door. "Be free in mirth; soon we'll drink a measure the table round!"

He lingered a moment, making certain that the crowd's attention was enticed by the meal before them, then turned with casual purpose and stepped through the door.

In the dimly lit, narrow corridor behind, the King stated in a flat tone, "There's blood on your face."

The young murderer blinked, then rubbed at his cheeks and forehead, searching for the offending stain. "It is Banquo's then."

A smile of deep satisfaction spread across Macbeth's lips. "It is better on your face than within him. Is he dispatched?"

The murderer nodded with vigor. "My Lord, his throat is cut; that I did for him."

Macbeth sighed, his entire bearing now relaxed. "You are the *best* of the cutthroats." He chuckled. "Yet he's also good that did the same for Fleance – if you did it, you are without equal."

The murderer swallowed hard, and Macbeth noted the hesitation in an instant. "Most royal sir ... Fleance is escaped."

For a moment, Macbeth did not move, did not react, did not even appear to breathe – the young man had to wonder if the King had heard his words ...

... then Macbeth turned partially away from the murderer, his shoulders sagging in a fashion that in no way resembled his prior relief.

"Then comes my fit of fear again," he whispered. "I would otherwise have been perfect – whole as the marble, immovable as the rock, as free and unconfined as the surrounding air." He clenched his fists. "But now I am cabined, cribbed, confined, bound in to insistent doubts and fears." He fell silent for another moment, staring at nothing. Then he regarded the murderer once more. "But Banquo's safe?"

The cutthroat again hurried to nod. "Aye, my good Lord! He bides safe in a ditch, with twenty trenched gashes on his head – the *least* gash a death to nature."

Macbeth forced an absent smile. "Thanks for *that*. There the grown serpent lies; the young worm that's fled has nature that, in time, will breed venom ... but no teeth for the present." He considered this for several long seconds, then shook himself and addressed the murderer once more. "Get you gone; tomorrow we'll confer again."

The murderer offered a swift bow, then retreated in equal haste.

"My royal Lord ...?"

Macbeth turned to find his Queen standing in the doorway; he struggled to assume a closed expression.

"You do not give the cheer of the proper host," she said. "The feast that is not often assured is little better than a purchased meal – while it is a-making, it is given with frequent *welcome*. To eat at home were best; if away from home, the sauce for the meat is *ceremony* – meals are bare without it."

Forcing a smile so wide that it fairly hurt his cheeks, Macbeth strode through the open doorway with a bawdy, "Sweet remembrancer!" All heads turned his way as he scooped up someone's wine goblet – for who would complain against the King? – and held it high in toast. "Now, good digestion wait on appetite, and health on both!"

After all had drunk in response, Lennox stood and called, "May it please Your Highness sit?" He gestured toward the seat Macbeth had indicated before.

Macbeth nodded, but rather than move to the table, he raised his purloined goblet once more. "Here we would now have all our country's nobility under one roof, were the graced person of our Banquo present – who may I rather charge with unkindness than pity for mischance!"

"His absence, sir," Ross responded, "lays blame upon his promise." More laughter; more cups raised; more wine drunk. Then Ross made his own attempt, actually moving toward the middle of the guests' tables. "If it please Your Highness, to grace us with your royal company."

Macbeth turned, and a small frown of irritation formed when he noted that all seats were taken. Had he not specifically declared that he would sit in the middle of the table? Was he expected to wait while others shuffled to make room?

Still, he recalled his self-given, self-serving duty for this evening, and kept his tone light as he commented, "The table's full."

Lennox rushed to join Ross. "Here is a place reserved, sir." They both stood, expectant, on either side of an occupied seat.

Macbeth was sincerely perplexed. "Where?"

Lennox looked equally confused. "*Here*, my good Lord."

A hairsbreadth from demanding an explanation, Macbeth noted that the resident of the stool in question had begun to turn around, as though finally noticing that his space was being offered without his knowledge. What poor nobleman were these two trying to—?

Macbeth's eyes widened and his jaw dropped. The goblet fell from his hand, splashing the remaining wine at his feet.

Concerned, Lennox asked, "What is it that moves Your Highness?"

Macbeth could not speak at first. He could only gape as the filthy, mutilated, blue-faced figure of Banquo turned to confront him – his horror, already considerable, mounted when he saw that one of Banquo's eyes had been ruptured, its swollen, maimed socket sagging empty, like a second atrocious mouth.

The King's breath returned, but he could only whisper, "Which of you have done this?"

The crowd murmured and looks of bewilderment were exchanged. Several asked, "What, my good Lord?"

Macbeth pointed at Banquo, some defiance growing within his fear. "You cannot say *I* did it! Never shake your gory locks at *me*!"

Ross, upon seeing his King bellowing toward an empty spot at the table, attempted to seize some control of the situation. "Gentlemen, rise," he called out, "his Highness is not well—"

"*Sit*, worthy friends!" the Queen cut him off. She hurried to stand before her trembling husband, her back to him as she addressed the room. "My Lord is often thus," she explained, "and has been from his youth. I pray you, keep seated. The fit is momentary; upon a thought he will again be well. If you note him too much, you shall worsen him and prolong his attack." She gestured to the mounds of food. "Feed, and regard him not."

For a long moment, the crowd of guests hesitated –

longing to follow Ross' advice and leave this bizarre scene, to remove themselves from the sight of their gasping, wild-eyed King, but also reluctant to aggrieve their Queen. At last, they bowed to the conditioning of rank, and resumed their seats and their meal.

When she was certain she had reined them in, Lady Macbeth turned and served her husband a scathing look. "Are you a *man*?" she spat under her breath.

Macbeth still trembled, his eyes still boggled, but he had gotten his racing breath under control, and his voice remained strong enough as he whispered back, "Aye, and a bold one, that dare look on *that* ..." He jerked his chin toward the open seat. "... which might appal the Devil."

Lady Macbeth scoffed, "Oh, fine stuff!" She glanced over her shoulder at their guests, ensuring that none were close enough to hear, then scolded, "This is the very painting of your *fear*; this is the air-drawn dagger which you said led you to Duncan." She shook her head. "Oh, these outbursts and starts – impostors next to *true* fear – would well befit a woman's story at a winter's fire, authorized by her *grandma*. Shame itself!" When she noted that Macbeth was still looking past her, over her shoulder toward the open seat at the table, with his mouth once more huffing like a beached fish, she took her husband's chin in her hand and forced him to meet her frustrated gaze. "Why do you make such faces? When all's done, you look but on *an empty stool*."

"Prithee," he implored, "see *there*!" He pointed past her. "Behold! Look! *See*!"

The guests grew uncomfortable once more as Macbeth pushed past her and addressed the open space at the table; all those near inched away, struggling – as best they could – to follow their Queen's advice to ignore the King's behavior.

"How say you?" Macbeth demanded of the air. "Why, what care I? If you can nod, then speak, too!" His face stretched into a rictus of a grin. "If charnel houses and our graves must send those that we bury back, then our tombs shall be the maws of birds of prey!"

A heavy hush followed the King's words as they echoed through the hall, and the King slowly grew conscious of that hush. He blinked at the now-empty seat a few times, his demeanor relaxing the slightest bit, before his gaze shifted left and right, seeing all those who dared not meet his eye, but whom he knew to be staring at him nonetheless.

"What, quite unmanned by your folly?" his wife whispered from behind him.

He turned on her in defiance, but kept his voice equally low. "As I stand here, I *saw* him."

"Fie," she hissed, "for shame!"

Macbeth slumped, defeated. Keeping his back to all those judging eyes – and yet, who were *they* to judge *him*?! – he murmured to his wife, "Blood has been shed before now, in the olden time, before human law purged the now-gentle commonwealth; aye, and since, too, murders have been performed too terrible for the ear. The times have been that, when the brains were out, the man would *die*, and there it would end. But now they *rise* again, with twenty mortal wounds on their crowns, and push us from our stools." He shook his hanging head, and shuddered. "This is more strange than such a murder is."

Dismissing the pure content of his words, Lady Macbeth – also painfully aware of those around them – instead evaluated his mood. He had just stated that he "saw" the specter, past tense, and spoke with improved lucidity. Perhaps the evening could still be salvaged?

With a somewhat raised voice, she said, "My worthy

Lord, your noble friends do miss you."

Macbeth looked her in the eye, and understood what she was attempting. Clearing his throat, he followed her lead. "I do forget." He faced their guests. "Do not wonder at me, my most worthy friends; I have a strange infirmity, which is nothing to those that know me." He strode forward and, again, seized the nearest goblet in disregard of its owner. "Come, love and health to all, then I'll sit down. Give me some wine, fill full."

Three different servants scrambled to fill their King's cup, after which he held it high, drawing a deep breath to present his toast ...

... and once more, he froze, his eyes widening as he gaped again at the same empty seat. For indeed, to his eyes, *Banquo had returned*.

Lady Macbeth saw the change in her husband, and barely contained her moan, dreading what might come next.

To his credit and her relief, Macbeth kept his voice steady, for the most part, as he declared, "I drink to the general joy of the whole table, and to our dear friend *Banquo*, whom we miss." His next words were directed, quite deliberately, to the empty stool. "I wish he were here!"

Lady Macbeth's shoulders fell as she finally understood exactly who it was her husband thought he saw. If only she could have known how this whole business would spiral so out of her control ...

"To all," Macbeth cried with too much vigor, "and *him*, we drink – and *all* drink to *all*!"

"Our duties, and the pledge," the Lords replied, with less enthusiasm than their King.

Once more cups raised, once more wine was drunk ... and Macbeth could no longer hold his nerve when the specter that wore Banquo's face stood and pointed a ghastly, accusing finger at him.

"*Away!*" he screamed, and flung his goblet at the phantom; a Lord on the opposite side of the table cried out when the cup struck him, but Macbeth was past hearing it. "And leave my sight! Let the earth hide you! Your bones are *marrowless*, your blood is *cold*; you have no *sight* in those eyes which you do glare with!"

Lady Macbeth's panic over how to best handle this disaster left her dizzy. "Think of this, good peers," she gasped, "as but a ... strange custom. It is no more!" She shot her husband a biting glare. "Only it spoils the pleasure of the time."

The nobles looked to one another, all searching for advice on how to handle this, and finding none.

Oblivious to it all, Macbeth stood strong against the apparition that plagued him. "What any man dares, *I* dare! If you approach me in the likeness of the rugged Russian bear, the armored rhinoceros, or the Hyrcanian tiger near the Caspian sea ..." He pointed at the spirit. "Take *any* shape but *that*, and my firm nerves shall never tremble!" He then grinned with hostility and challenge. "Or be *alive* again, and dare me to a deserted place with your sword – if my body trembles then, proclaim me a *baby girl*."

Dismissing Macbeth's bravado and ultimatum, the image of Banquo surged forward, sending the King cowering backward, his arms flung before him in impotent defense.

"Go hence, horrible shadow!" Macbeth cried, nearly losing his footing in his hasty retreat, "Unreal mockery, *go hence!*" He huddled in on himself, waiting for those ghoulish, cold hands to seize him, to close around his throat, to rend his flesh, to ... to ...

When no such fate befell him, Macbeth slowly opened his tearing eyes and dropped his shaking arms.

Nothing. The ghost was gone.

In an instant, his tears dried and his trembling ceased. He looked down at his hands, pleased to see they no longer shook.

"Why, look so ..." he commented aloud, "... being gone, I am a man again." He smiled, then looked up at the gaping, shuffling, unnerved crowd before him. Somehow, he managed to keep his smile in place. "Pray you, sit still."

In a soft but heavy voice, Lady Macbeth spoke for all. "You have displaced the mirth, broke the good meeting ... with most admired disorder."

Looking around at all their gawking faces, Macbeth opened his mouth to speak, lost his words, then swallowed and tried again. "Can such things be," he asked, gesturing toward the empty seat, "and pass over us like a sudden summer's cloud, without our special wonder?" He swept the same hand around the room. "You make me a stranger to my own disposition, when now I think you can behold such *sights* and keep the natural ruby of your cheeks, when mine are blanched with fear."

Ross took a very hesitant step forward. "What 'sights,' my Lord?"

The Queen answered before Macbeth could speak further. "I pray you, speak not. He grows worse and worse, and questions enrage his condition." She spared Macbeth a quick glance of staged evaluation, then shook her head. "To all at once, good night. Stand not upon the ceremonious order of your going, but *go*." When they did not instantly move, she snapped, "At once!"

One and all – Lords and Ladies, nobles and servants

– they hurried to leave the dining hall. Only Lennox took the time to say to her, "Good night, and better health attend His Majesty!"

Lady Macbeth nodded her acknowledgment, but it was dismissive. "A kind goodnight to all!"

At last, to the King's casual observation and the Queen's deepest relief, they were alone; even their own castle servants had leaped upon the opportunity to vacate the hall. With a heavy sigh, he sat upon the very stool which had centered within his emotional maelstrom; after several long, quiet seconds, she sat beside him.

Another stretch of silence passed before Macbeth said, "It will have blood, they say; 'blood will have blood.' Gravestones have been known to move and trees to speak; omens and revealed relations have – by scavenging magpies and jackdaw crows and chattering rooks – exposed the secretest murderer." He shook his head, then asked his wife, "What is the time of night?"

Lady Macbeth, who had been idly rubbing her hands together as she stared into space, blinked in confusion for a moment, then glanced at the nearest window. "Almost at odds with morning," she replied with a tired shrug, "which is which."

Macbeth nodded in understanding. Morning, night ... which was which, indeed, to those such as they had become? Rather than wander down that dismal, cyclical path, however, he changed the subject. "What do you say, that *Macduff* denies us his company, despite my great bidding?"

Again, Lady Macbeth shrugged, so exhausted she could barely follow this shift in the conversation. "Did you send to him, sir?"

"I hear it indirectly; but I will send to him." He gestured in the general direction the many noblemen had fled minutes before. "There's not a one of them but, in his house, I keep a paid servant."

Once again, heavy silence stretched between them as they sat together, not quite huddling.

Finally, Macbeth told her, in a very soft voice, "I will tomorrow – and very early I will – go to the Weïrd Sisters." He saw Lady Macbeth stiffen, but when she said nothing, he continued. "More shall they speak; for now I am determined to know, by the worst means, the worst to come. For mine own good, all other consideration shall give way."

He looked down at his hands, and in his mind's eye, they were hardly clean; little did he suspect how well his wife would empathize.

"I have stepped in blood so far that, even if I should wade no further, returning would be as tedious as going over. Strange things I have in head that will come to hand, which must be acted upon before they may be considered."

At last, Lady Macbeth turned to face him. She looked as drained as he felt. "You lack the preservative of all natures – *sleep*."

Macbeth could not deny that. He put his arm around her shoulders, perhaps the softest touch that had passed between them since this dark business began.

"Come," he agreed, "we'll go to sleep. My strange self-delusion is the fear of the inexperienced that wants *hardening* use – we are still young in criminal deeds."

To that, Lady Macbeth said nothing.

PART THREE

CHAPTER FIVE [1]

In that very same time of the night being at odds with the morning, the Weïrd Sisters of whom Macbeth spoke gathered once more upon their heath. Lightning struck and thunder rumbled, though no rain fell – and without warning, their goddess, Hecate, loomed over them.

The witches bowed before her. Unlike their grotesque selves, Hecate was quite beautiful at first glance. Any prolonged observer, however, might note how tall she was, how her eyes gleamed with a sickening, urine-colored shine, how her hair was so coarse as to draw blood if stroked the wrong direction.

The sisters, familiar with her appearance, were more concerned with the evident anger upon her visage.

---

[1]

The majority of scholars suspect that Act III, Scene V of Macbeth *is a spurious interpolation, taken from a musical by Thomas Middleton,* The Witch *(1610). Almost all film or theatre presentations omit the scene altogether; indeed, there is a song near the end that neither the Riverside Shakespeare nor the Yale Shakespeare editions included in the play's text, but only in the closing Textual Notes. I have included this material as Part Three, Chapter Five (sans the song) in the spirit of completion.*

"Why, what is the matter, Hecate?" the first sister asked, her tone full of false innocence. *"You look angry."*

Hecate was neither fooled nor amused. She spoke, her singsong voice – like her looks – appealing at first, but grating on the ear as her speech lengthened.

> "HAVE I NOT REASON, UGLY HAGS AS YOU
>   ARE?
> SAUCY AND OVERBOLD? HOW DID YOU DARE
> TO TRADE AND TRAFFIC WITH MACBETH
> IN RIDDLES AND AFFAIRS OF DEATH;
> AND I, THE MISTRESS OF YOUR CHARMS,
> THE SECRET CONTRIVER OF ALL HARMS,
> WAS NEVER CALLED TO BEAR MY PART,
> OR SHOW THE GLORY OF OUR ART?"

The three witches huddled together, each struggling not to cower outright, as their goddess continued in growing anger.

> "AND, WHICH IS WORSE, ALL YOU HAVE DONE
> HAS BEEN BUT FOR A WAYWARD SON,
> SPITEFUL AND WRATHFUL, WHO, AS OTHERS
>   DO,
> LOVES FOR HIS OWN ENDS, NOT FOR YOU."

The sisters nodded, and groveled. This pleased Hecate, who resumed her verse with less heat.

> "BUT MAKE AMENDS NOW. GET YOU GONE,
> AND AT HELL'S RIVER OF ACHERON
> MEET ME IN THE MORNING. THERE HE
> WILL COME TO KNOW HIS DESTINY."

Hecate gestured toward their cauldron.

> "YOUR VESSELS AND YOUR SPELLS PROVIDE,
> YOUR CHARMS AND EVERYTHING BESIDE.
> I AM FOR THE AIR; THIS NIGHT I'LL SPEND

UNTO A DISMAL AND A FATAL END."

She pointed into the brightening sky.

"GREAT BUSINESS MUST BE WROUGHT BEFORE
    NOON.
UPON THE CORNER OF THE MOON
THERE HANGS A VAPOROUS DROP PROFOUND;
I'LL CATCH IT BEFORE IT COME TO GROUND;
AND THAT DISTILLED BY MAGIC SLEIGHTS,
SHALL RAISE SUCH CUNNING SPRITES
AS BY THE STRENGTH OF THEIR ILLUSION
SHALL DRAW HIM ON TO HIS RUIN."

Hecate smiled, an endearing and unsettling sight.

"HE SHALL SPURN FATE, SCORN DEATH, AND
    BEAR
HIS HOPES ABOVE WISDOM, GRACE AND FEAR;
AND YOU ALL KNOW, OVERCONFIDENT
SECURITY
IS MORTALS' WORST ENEMY."

The earth beneath their feet rumbled as the very first fingers of dawn touched the world, and a faraway voice seemed to cry: "Come away ... come away ..."

Hecate noted it at once.

"HARK! I AM CALLED; MY LITTLE SPIRIT, SEE,
SITS IN A FOGGY CLOUD, AND STAYS FOR ME."

And with that she was gone, fading like a night's dream upon the light of morning.

The first sister turned to her siblings at once. "Come, let's make haste. She'll soon be back again."

And they proceeded with their business.

Sometime later, far from the heath where the witches skulked – but only a short distance from the palace at Forres, where the increasingly erratic and savage King Macbeth ruled with a tightening fist – Lennox sauntered through the field behind his home. A fellow Scottish lord, recently returned from England, strode in his company, and Lennox had grown uncomfortable of late carrying any "delicate" conversations within his own walls. He had no solid evidence, of course, that members of his staff were listening with perked ears, and yet ...

And yet.

Glancing around as they walked, reassuring himself – as he had several times over this young morning – Lennox continued conversing with his fellow Lord. "My former speeches have coincided with your thoughts, which you can interpret farther; only, I say, things have been strangely managed. The gracious Duncan was pitied by Macbeth – marry, *after* he was dead."

A falcon cried in the distance, bringing them both up short. Lennox shook his head, and his tone grew more and more sarcastic as he pressed on.

"And the right-valiant Banquo walked too late; whom, you may say – if it please you – *Fleance* killed, for Fleance fled. Men must not walk too late. Who can avoid the thought of how monstrous it was for Malcolm and for Donalbain to kill their gracious father? Damned crime! How it did *grieve* Macbeth! Did he not straight, in pious rage, tear the two delinquents, that were the slaves of drink and thralls of sleep? Was *that* not nobly done?" Lennox shook his head again in disgust. "Aye, and *wisely,* too; for it would have angered any heart alive to hear the men deny it. So that, I say, he has borne all things well ... and I do think that, if he had Duncan's sons under his key – as, if it please Heaven, he shall *not* – they should find what it were to kill a father; so should Fleance."

Lennox heaved a heavy, wearisome sigh as he slowed his pace, then stopped. The Lord stood with him.

"But, peace!" Lennox said, to himself more than his companion. "For from outspoken words, and 'cause he failed his presence at the tyrant's feast, I hear Macduff lives in disgrace." He looked around once more, then asked his companion in a low voice, "Sir, can you tell where Malcolm bestows himself?"

The Lord took his own survey of their surroundings as he spoke just as low. "The son of Duncan – from whom this tyrant holds the due of his birth – lives in the English court, and is received by the most pious King Edward the Confessor with such grace that the malevolence of his misfortune takes nothing from the high respect he receives."

Lennox nodded. It made sense; Edward the Confessor had himself spent time in exile, in Normandy, so it went without saying that he would empathize with Malcolm's plight.

"There Macduff has gone to beseech the holy King on Malcolm's behalf," the Lord continued, "to wake the people of Northumberland and Malcolm's uncle Siward, their warlike Earl, that, by the help of these – with God above to ratify the work – we may again give meat to our banquet tables, sleep to our nights, free our feasts and banquets from bloody knives, do sincere homage and receive freely-given honors, *all* which we pine for now." Then the Lord's face tightened as he added, "And this report has so exasperated King Macbeth that he prepares for some attempt of *war*."

"Did he send to Macduff?"

"He did; and when Macduff gave an absolute 'Sir, not I,' the scowling messenger turned his back, and said 'humph,' as one should say 'You'll rue the time that hampers me with this answer.'"

Lennox mused that the poor messenger probably dreaded Macbeth's reaction to such a reply. But his chief concern was for his fellow nobleman. "And that well might advise Macduff to a caution, to hold what distance his wisdom can provide." His gaze drifted skyward. "May some holy angel fly to the court of England and unfold this message before Macduff comes, that a swift blessing may soon return him to this, our country suffering under a hand accursed!"

The Lord sighed heavily and touched Lennox's slumped shoulder. "I'll send my prayers with him."

Indeed, they prayed together.

Part Four

Chapter One

Thunder rolled across the land once more, as it always did when the followers of Hecate practiced their ominous craft. The vibration shook the earth and echoed through a dim cavern near their familiar heath. Flames flickered beneath their boiling cauldron, which churned in the center, sending twisted, shifting shadow puppets dancing across the bedewed walls.

The last vestiges of the booming reverberation trailed off just as the three witches gathered around the large cauldron.

The first of the witches proclaimed, "Thrice the brindled cat has mewed."

The second declared, "Thrice and once the hedgehog whined."

The third, "The harpy cries, ' 'Tis time, 'tis time.' "

The sisters nodded as one. Then they huddled closer to the cauldron, and the first began their work with:

"Round about the cauldron go;
In the poisoned entrails throw.
Toad, that under cold stone
Days and nights has thirty-one
Exuded venom sleeping got,
Boil you first in the charmed pot."

The first produced the toad from the folds of her

dirty, ragged robe, and tossed it, still living, into the boiling broth. Then the three joined hands and chanted:

"Double, double, toil and trouble;
Fire burn, and cauldron bubble."

Their hands dropped, and the second leaned forward:

"Fillet of a swamp snake,
In the cauldron boil and bake;
Eye of newt and toe of frog,
Wool of bat and tongue of dog,
Adder's forked tongue and reptile's sting,
Lizard's leg and owlet's wing;
For a charm of powerful trouble,
Like a Hell-broth boil and bubble."

She dumped the aforementioned contents from her tattered bag, then the sisters locked hands again.

"Double, double, toil and trouble;
Fire burn, and cauldron bubble."

Their hands dropped, and the third sister took her turn; unlike her siblings, however, she tossed each item into the Hell-broth as she named them:

"Scale of dragon, tooth of wolf,
Witches' mummy flesh, mouth and gulf
Of the glutinous salt-sea shark;
Root of hemlock dug in the dark;
Liver of blaspheming Jew,
Gall of goat, and slips of yew
Sliced off in the moon's eclipse;
Nose of Turk, and Tartar's lips;
Finger of birth-strangled babe
Ditch-delivered by a whoring drab,
Make the gruel thick and tough as slab.
Add thereto a tiger's innard-chaudron,
For the ingredients of our cauldron."

She finished at last, and their hands locked once more.

"Double, double, toil and trouble;
Fire burn and cauldron bubble."

And the first and last sister bowed their heads as the second now poured in the final ingredient of their Hell-broth:

"Cool it with a baboon's blood;
Then the charm is firm and good."

Thunder rumbled once more, but this time it originated from within the earth itself. The sisters turned as one to find their cavern now occupied by their goddess, Hecate; they were not, however, expecting to see three *other* witches in her company, but the Weïrd Sisters knew better than to voice or express any hint of displeasure.

Hecate stepped forward, looming over them but with a serpentine smile upon her lips:

"OH, WELL DONE! I COMMEND YOUR PAINS,
AND EVERY ONE SHALL SHARE IN THE GAINS.
AND NOW ABOUT THE CAULDRON SING,
LIVE ELVES AND FAIRIES IN A RING,
ENCHANTING ALL THAT YOU PUT IN." [2]

Hecate threw her hands into the air, the Weïrd Sisters

---

[2]

Similar to Act III, Scene V, many scholars question the validity of Hecate's appearance in this scene. Likewise, a song called Black Spirits *can be found in some Textual Notes, but neither the Riverside Shakespeare nor the Yale Shakespeare editions included it in the play's main text; the song is again suspected to have originated from Thomas Middleton's* The Witch.

awaited their blessing ... but just as suddenly as she had arrived, the witch goddess and her company were gone.

The three sisters exchanged looks of confusion all around. Had they offended their mistress? Why would—?

Then the second sister's back stiffened:

"By the pricking of my thumbs, something *wicked* this way comes."

A hammering echoed through the cavern, but this time it was clearly of mortal origin; it smacked of the hilt of a sword pounding upon the stony entrance.

The second sister shared the briefest smile with her siblings before calling out, "Open, locks, whoever knocks!"

Not a heartbeat passed before Macbeth stepped into their domain, sword in hand.

The King of Scotland was in a foul mood. Too much time had he already wasted in search of these Weïrd Sisters. He had indeed left early the morning after the disastrous gathering in the dining hall ... and the morning after that ... and the morning after that! He had located the heath, and though some instinct had insisted he would find those he sought in that place, he did not. But where else to look? So he returned there on each attempt – followed by a King's guard who gave him furtive looks that spoke volumes to their private judgement of his behavior! – to spiral further and further outward, seeking some sign of those strange women ... and only today did he achieve satisfaction.

But lost time could not be regained, and so that satisfaction was tainted.

"How now, you secret, black, and midnight hags!" he grumbled in a heavy tone that would have unnerved his soldiering kinsmen – yet the sisters merely looked at him with the vaguest of smiles. Petulant, he snapped, "What is it you do?"

As one, they answered, "A deed without a name."

Macbeth strode further into the cavern, sheathing his sword but keeping his hand upon the hilt. "*I* conjure *you*, by that demonic art which you profess – however you come to know it – answer me." He loomed over them, willing the women to bow before his temper. "Though you untie the winds and let them fight against the churches; though the frothy waves confound and swallow sailors up; though ripe wheat be beaten flat and trees blown down; though castles topple on their warders' heads; though palaces and pyramids do slope their heads to their foundations; though the treasure of nature's seeds tumble all together, even till destruction's satisfaction ... *answer me* to what I ask you!"

The first: "Speak."

The second: "Demand."

The third: "We'll answer."

Macbeth blinked; their easy acquiescence daunted him in a way that open resistance would not. Could they have been expecting him all along? Surely not, surely they could not—

And yet, that was the very reason he sought them, the very skill he required.

The eldest witch stepped closer, until she was close enough to embrace – a sickening thought, that; her breath smelled like horse sweat.

"Say," she spoke in a husky voice, "if you would rather hear it from our mouths, or from our *masters*'?"

Macbeth hesitated for only the briefest moment, then thrust his chin forward and stated, "Call them; let me see them."

The first witch nodded and returned to her sisters, as

they all gathered around the cauldron. "Pour in sow's blood," she instructed her brethren, "that has eaten her nine young; throw grease that's sweated from the murderer's gallows into the flame."

The second and third witches did so in turn, then they all linked hands and said together:

"Come, high or low;
Thy self and function deftly show!"

Once more thunder of the earth boomed; Macbeth dropped into a defensive posture, ready to draw his blade, but the witches did not react.

Then, an image appeared to rise from the steam of the boiling cauldron. Macbeth squinted at the apparition, at first unable to make out any detail and thinking perhaps it was another trick of his mind's eye ... but then it pulsed with inner, cold light and solidified into the visage of an armored, disembodied *head*, its visor down but its eye-slits betraying the darkness within.

By shear fortitude, Macbeth released his sword and pronounced in a firm voice, "Tell me, you unknown power—"

But the first witch cut him off:

"He knows your thought: Hear his speech, but speak nought."

And then the armored head pulsed with light again, and spoke for itself:

"MACBETH! MACBETH! MACBETH! ... BEWARE MACDUFF, BEWARE THE THANE OF FIFE. DISMISS ME. ENOUGH."

And with those curt words, the head descended back into the cauldron.

Macbeth released the breath he had not realized he was holding. The speech had been brief indeed, yet it had touched upon the proper nerve. "Whatever you are," he said, "for your good caution, thanks; you have rightly harped the very tune of my fear." He reached out toward the cauldron. "But one word more—"

To his shock, the first sister slapped his hand away. "He will not be commanded." And as he bristled in deadly indignation, she continued, "Here's another, more potent than the first."

The second apparition snapped up into view much faster, and its nature was more disconcerting than the bodiless head. It was a child, a *bloody* child – a boy, so it seemed – smeared with gore, his limbs drawn inward, his eyes sunken. But when he spoke, his voice was pitched like a grown man, with a quality that reminded Macbeth instantly of Macduff himself.

"MACBETH!" it cried. "MACBETH! MACBETH!"

"Had I three ears," Macbeth replied, humble but also impatient to get on with it, "I'd hear you."

"BE BLOODY, BOLD, AND RESOLUTE – LAUGH TO SCORN THE POWER OF MAN ... FOR NONE OF WOMAN BORN SHALL HARM MACBETH."

And the grisly child dropped back into the Hell-broth as fast as he had arisen.

Macbeth sighed, his heart feeling so light he was nearly giddy. No one of woman born shall harm him? Why, that was the entire human race! When he spoke, his words were colored with laughter of relief.

"Then live, Macduff;" he cried, "why need I fear you?" He thought a moment. "But yet I'll make assurance double sure, and take a guaranty of fate: *You shall not live*, so that I may tell my pale-hearted fear that it lies, and sleep in spite of thunder."

The irony of his poor choice of words was not lost on Macbeth as the cavern shook with the heaviest earthen rumble yet. A third apparition rose from the cauldron, this one another child, but older. The ghastly pale skin of his face shimmered beneath a sparkling crown upon his head, and in his left hand – to keep his sword hand free, as it were? – he brandished a thin branch; no, more than just a branch, more like a bough.

When the third phantom said nothing at first, Macbeth demanded of the witches, "What *is* this that rises like the offspring of a King, and wears upon his baby-brow the round and top of sovereignty?"

The sisters spoke in a singular voice: "Listen, but speak not to it."

As if that were his cue, the crowned boy spoke. "BE LION-METTLED, PROUD, AND TAKE NO CARE WHO CHAFES, WHO FRETS, OR WHERE CONSPIRERS ARE: MACBETH SHALL NEVER BE VANQUISHED ... UNTIL GREAT BIRNAM WOOD SHALL COME TO HIGH DUNSINANE HILL AGAINST HIM."

And with that, the third apparition melted back into the cauldron.

Macbeth's heart swelled with such jubilance, even the sight of the Weïrd Sisters no longer made his skin crawl. A *forest*, traveling a dozen miles from near Perth to the crag of Dunsinane?

"That will *never* be!" he exhaled. "Who can draft the forest, bid the tree unfix his earth-bound root? Sweet prophecies! Good!" He clapped his hands. "Rebellious dead, never rise till the wood of Birnam rises, and our high-placed Macbeth shall live the full lease of natural life, paying his breath only to time and mortal custom!"

The most rational part of Macbeth knew that he had learned what he wanted, that he should now turn his back to the three witches and leave this noisome place forever...

... and yet, still – *still* – he somehow wasn't fully

satisfied, wasn't content in his safety and standing as King. Therefore, he spoke further.

"Yet my heart throbs to know one thing: Tell me, if your art can tell so much ... shall Banquo's descendants ever reign in this Kingdom?"

Again, the sisters spoke as one: "Seek to know no more."

Any reluctance Macbeth might have felt over soliciting additional foreknowledge burned away in the heat of his anger – who were these creatures to deny *him*, the King of Scotland, anything which he desired?

"I will be satisfied!" he snapped. "Deny me this, and an eternal curse fall on you! Let me know—" He cut himself off as his eyes drifted past them. When he spoke again, it was with less certainty. "Why sinks that cauldron? And what music is this?"

Indeed, the cauldron appeared to be lowering into the fire beneath it, and he swore he heard hautboys playing the ceremonial procession that announced his royal presence before the court, and that of Duncan's before him, but the musical notes felt too heavy and flat. The flames flickered and crackled with increased fervor as the cauldron all but disappeared, a massive cloud of billowing, pulsing, writhing steam stretching out and around. Shadows danced through the eerie vapor and along the walls of the cavern.

Macbeth withdrew a step, but no further.

"Show!" the first witch cried, followed by her sisters in turn.

"Show!"

"Show!"

Then, together:

"Show his eyes, and grieve his heart;
Come like shadows, so depart!"

Macbeth gasped as a crystalline figure appeared from within the vapor. The image of a man scarcely beyond his boyhood, he strutted before Macbeth even while standing still, not deigning to meet his eye – if he were capable, as his own eyes were solid white, more like those of statues than any living being. He wore crown and robes, and carried an elaborate, royal scepter.

Macbeth had never before seen the likeness of this young shadow-King, yet he would recognize the influence upon those features anywhere. "You are too like the spirit of Banquo," Macbeth spat, willing himself not to cower, with partial success. "Down!"

The phantom obeyed his command, dropped suddenly back into flames under the melted cauldron. But Macbeth was granted no relief as a second, similar young King of undeniable shared heritage took his place.

"Your crown does sear my eyeballs," Macbeth whispered, "and your hair, your other gold-bound brow, is like the first ..."

Then the second young man dropped away, only to be replaced by another.

Macbeth moaned in spite of himself. "A third is like the former ..."

Finally, he could stand no more – but what to do? Draw his sword against a being of vapor? So instead, he whirled upon the sisters.

"Filthy hags! Why do you show me this?"

The witches cared nothing for his impotent anger, but merely stood in silence. And so Macbeth felt his attention drawn back to the latest shadow, crown and scepter ever in place.

"A fourth! Start, eyes!" His hand sought to cover his face, yet he could not look away as the procession continued with a fifth figure.

"What, will the line stretch out to the crack of doom? ... Another yet! ... A seventh!" He shook his head. "I'll see no more ... and yet the *eighth* appears, who bears a mirror – which shows me *many* more; and some I see that carry two-fold balls and treble scepters. Horrible sight!"

The notion of the dual-balled scepters, which indicated one who was King of both Scotland and England, and the triple staff, which signified a King of Scotland and England *and* Ireland, was too much for Macbeth. He buckled, yearning to turn away from the tortuous view, yet finding himself unable to do so – was it a curse of the sisters, or his own morbid desire for self-flagellation which locked him so? He did not know.

Either way, Macbeth gaped on, and so confronted the final specter of this prophetic procession.

"Now I see it is true ..." he whispered, "... for Banquo – his hair blood-clotted still – smiles upon me, and points at them for his own."

Banquo – with a grin of deep satisfaction upon his bloody face, damn him! – was indeed the final sight to greet him. The steam surged, the vapor rushed inward rather than outward, and the image of Banquo and the lingering shadows of his long line of descendants vanished.

Moving slowly, the shock of Scotland's future having numbed him from head to toe, Macbeth turned toward the sisters. "What? Is this so?"

The first witch stepped forward. "Aye, sir, all this is so. But why does Macbeth stand thus as in a trance?" She turned to her siblings:

"Come, sisters, cheer we up his sprites,
And show the best of our delights.
I'll charm the air to give a sound,
While you perform your antic round,

That this great King may kindly say,
Our duties did his welcome pay."

Music again surged through the air, and the sisters – with surprising grace – twirled around and toward one another, closer and closer, until they almost danced upon the rim of the molten cauldron itself ...

... and in a breath, they, too, were gone. [3]

Macbeth spun around in a stupor. Not only had the Weïrd Sisters disappeared, but all the steam from the cauldron as well; in fact, the cauldron had returned to its former self, unmelted and with no sign of fire beneath its belly.

Where are they? Gone? He spat upon the cavern's floor in disgust. *Let this pernicious hour stand forever accursed in the calendar!*

The sound of horses galloping nearby brought him erect with a jolt; he was startled to realize that he had been conscious of no sounds from outside this damned cave since he set foot inside. But now he could hear his escorts talking amongst themselves.

If he could hear them speaking to one another ... perhaps his "privacy" had been nothing more than another illusion? And, if so, had his men without heard or seen anything untoward?

"Come in, without there!" he called, his tone sharp.

He heard shuffled footsteps and more talking, and a few moments later Lennox appeared, torch in hand, at the

---

[3]

The First Witch's farewell speech, as well as the three Witches' dance, is again questioned by scholars; this small section is considered by most to be another spurious addition to Shakespeare's original script.

mouth of the cavern.

"What's Your Grace's will?"

Macbeth watched him carefully as he asked, "Did you see the Weïrd Sisters?"

Lennox's expression was one of sincere bafflement. "No, my Lord."

"They came not by you?"

"No, indeed, my Lord."

Macbeth nodded. *Infected be the air whereon they ride, and damned all those that trust them!* He then asked, "I did hear the galloping of horses. Who was it came by?"

Lennox hesitated for the barest moment before answering, "It is two or three, my Lord, that bring you word: Macduff is fled to England."

Macbeth's sword hand seized the hilt of his blade. "Fled to England!"

"Aye, my good Lord."

Macbeth huffed in anger as he spun about and paced the cavern; Lennox, not yet dismissed, waited in patience.

Time, you anticipate my dread exploits: The fickle purpose is never overtook unless the deed occurs with it. From this moment, the very firstborn of my heart shall be the firstborn of my hand! He drew a determined breath. *And even now, to crown my thoughts with acts, be it thought and done: I will surprise the castle of Macduff, seize upon Fife, give to the edge of the sword his wife, his babes, and all unfortunate souls that follow him in his family line. No boasting like a fool – this deed I'll do before this purpose cool. But no more visions!*

At last, content in his renewed determination, Macbeth addressed Lennox. "Where are these gentlemen? Come, bring me where they are."

And he led the way out of the witches' cavern.

<h1 style="text-align: center;">Part Four</h1>

<h2 style="text-align: center;">Chapter Two</h2>

Lady Macduff was livid. She paced to and fro, unable to contain her indignation at this news Ross had brought of her husband – if "husband" was a suitable name for the unworthy coward! Flown to England, leaving her alone with their children ... what sort of "man" would do such a thing?!

Ross stood silent for the moment. When he had asked for a private word with Lady Macduff, she had escorted him here, to the family's common chamber of Macduff's castle in Fife. What Ross had not expected was for the Lady to allow her and Macduff's eldest son, still just a boy, to accompany them. Ross' hints that perhaps their words were not for the boy's ears had been either misunderstood or ignored. And so, with the boy sitting quietly in a nearby chair, he had delivered his unfortunate report.

Finally, the Lady spun on her heel and faced Ross once more. "What had he done," she demanded, "to make him fly the land?"

Ross bit his tongue at first; could she truly be so blind to the way things were under the reign of King Macbeth? Then, speaking carefully, he said, "You must have patience, madam—"

"*He* had none;" she snapped, "his flight was

madness. When our actions do not, our *fears* do make us look like traitors."

"You know not whether it was his *wisdom* or his fear."

Lady Macduff scoffed, "*Wisdom?* To leave his wife, to leave his babes, his mansion and his estates in a place from which he himself does fly? He loves us *not*, he lacks the natural touch of a husband and father – for the poor wren, the most diminutive of birds, will fight against the owl for her young ones in her nest!" She shook her head, her eyes full of abhorrence. "All is the fear and nothing is the love; as little is the 'wisdom,' where the flight so runs against all reason."

Ross flicked a glance toward the boy, but Macduff's son maintained a tranquil expression throughout – if only his mother would follow his example.

Approaching her slowly, his hands open and outward, Ross soothed, "My dearest cousin, I pray you control yourself." He took her gently but firmly by the shoulders, so that she should not turn away as he said, "But, for your husband, he is noble, wise, judicious, and best knows the disorders of the season."

Her face tightened, but she did not refute him.

Satisfied, he released her. "I dare not speak much further, but cruel are the times, when we are 'traitors' and do not know ourselves as such; when we credit rumor because of our fear, yet know not *what* we fear, but float upon a wild and violent sea each way and move—" He stopped, shaking his own head, saddened. Then he puffed out his chest in a false show of confidence. "I take my leave of you; it shall not be long before I'll be here again. Things at the worst will cease, or else climb upward to what they were before."

He waited for her to return his smile. She did not.

And so Ross turned to the boy instead, and ruffled his hair in a playful gesture. "My pretty cousin, blessing upon you!"

From behind, he heard Lady Macduff speak in a low voice, "Fathered he is, and yet he's fatherless."

Ross looked upon them both, then blinked a few times and cleared his throat. "I am so much a fool – should I stay longer, my tears would be my disgrace and your discomfort. I take my leave at once."

And so he left, leaving Lady Macduff in a whirlwind of emotion. She waited a moment to contain them – though perhaps not as long as she should have – before approaching her quiet son.

He looked up at her, expectant. He had heard every word, of course, and was old enough to understand it all for himself, and yet he looked to her for some final seal.

"Sirrah ..." she addressed him, the term less disdainful when used parent-to-child rather than master-to-servant.

The boy waited.

"Your father's dead," she said at last; when she continued, she spoke more to herself than to him, "and what will you do now? How will you live?"

After very brief consideration, the boy answered, "As birds do, Mother."

Lady Macduff could not resist smiling. "What, with worms and flies?"

"With what I get, I mean," he explained, "and so do they."

She knelt before him and touched his cheek. "Poor bird! You should never fear the net nor the birdlime trap, the pitfall nor the snare."

"Why should I, Mother? They are not set for 'poor' birds." He stared at his mother for a moment, then surprised her by stating, "My father is not dead, for all your saying."

"Yes, he is dead," she corrected, and she wanted to be firm. But how could she be, when the boy was correct in the literal sense? She touched his cheek again. "What will you do for a father?"

"No," he returned, "what will *you* do for a husband?"

With forced good cheer, she claimed, "Why, I can buy me twenty at any market."

"Then you'll buy 'em to sell again."

This time, despite the mood, she laughed aloud. "You speak with all your wit; and yet, in faith, with wit enough for your age."

Then, without warning, he asked, "Was my father a traitor, Mother?"

Lady Macduff's breath caught, but she answered him. "Aye, that he was."

Her son pondered this, then: "What *is* a 'traitor'?"

"Why, one that swears and lies."

"And be *all* traitors that do so?"

"Every one that does so is a traitor, and ..." She swallowed. "... must be hanged."

"And must they *all* be hanged that swear and lie?"

She nodded. "Every one."

"Who must hang them?"

"Why, the honest men."

He considered this as well, then the relentless boy stated, "Then the liars and swearers are fools, for there are liars and swearers enough to beat the honest men and hang up *them*."

More laughter escaped her; how could she help herself? "Now," she chuckled, giving a playful swat at his backside, "God help you for speaking so, poor monkey!"

The boy, too, laughed.

But the moment could not delay her unhappiness for long. She pulled him close, hugging him. "But what *will* you do for a father?" she whispered.

The boy pushed back so that he could speak to her face, but not so far as to leave her arms. "If he were dead, you'd weep for him; if you would not, it were a good sign that I should quickly have a new father."

"Poor prattler," she gasped in affected shock, "how you talk!"

But the bonding moment was broken as the door, through which Ross had departed so recently, flew open hard enough to slam into the wall. Lady Macduff's breath caught, and she pulled her son to her.

A middle-aged man, his poor clothing damp with sweat, his hair likewise plastered to his forehead, panted in deep huffs as he hurried toward them.

"Bless you, fair dame!" he sputtered even as she made to withdraw from him. "I am not known to you ... though I know well *your* state of honor ..." He tried to speak further, but he bent forward, his hands upon his knees as he fought for a deep breath.

Lady Macduff thought perhaps he was feverish and sick, but his condition smacked more of a man who had run a great distance without pause. She waited for him to continue, but she maintained her protective hold on her son.

When the messenger could again speak, he said, "I fear some danger does nearly approach you. If you will take a humble man's advice ... be *not* found here; go hence, with your little ones!" When her eyes widened, he gestured a quick apology. "Methinks I am too savage, to frighten you thus ... but to allow worse to come to you would be brutal cruelty – cruelty which is too near your person ...”

As if awaiting this cue, a scream echoed from somewhere else within the castle. Lady Macduff and her son were startled, to be sure, but the sound caused the messenger's face to go deathly pale.

“Heaven preserve you!” the man blurted as he raced back toward the open door. “I dare stay no longer!”

“Where should I fly?” Lady Macduff demanded of the retreating man. “I have done no harm!”

But the messenger was already gone, leaving her alone with her boy ... and the approaching sounds of further cries and violence.

But I remember now, followed her bleak thoughts, *I am in this earthly world, where to do harm is often laudable, and to do good sometimes accounted dangerous folly. Why then, alas, do I put up that womanly defense, to say 'I have done no harm'?*

Yet again, a form moved into the doorway of their common chamber, and for an instant, she thought the messenger had returned.

He had not.

Two men entered the room, and while the unknown, kind-hearted messenger had been dressed shabbily, he had not borne the hostility, the air of barbarism that hung over these men.

“Who are these faces?” she challenged, striving to maintain an air of authority, as if each of them did not hear the growing chaos and fear echoing throughout the castle.

The first man, the smaller and younger of the two intruders, approached her and asked, in a reasonable tone, “Where is your husband?”

“I hope,” she stated, looking down her nose at him – for she had nothing left in this moment but her dignity, "in no place so unsanctified where such as *you* may find him."

The intruder appeared more amused than insulted. "He's a traitor."

Without warning, Lady Macduff's son exploded from her sheltering arms, rushing the man. "You lie," the boy screamed, "you shag-haired villain!" And he tried to punch the hateful man in the groin.

But the boy's assault was both clumsy and obvious, and the man easily evaded harm by turning his hips. The boy drew back to hit him a second time, only to have the wrist seized and twisted around; somewhere within, a bone snapped audibly.

"What, you runt!" the intruder barked ...

... and in that moment between heartbeats, the dazed Lady Macduff realized she'd still had far more to lose than her mere dignity.

The intruder freed a dagger and plunged it deep into the boy's back. "Young spawn of treachery!" the man spat, pulling the blade out and flicking blood across Lady Macduff's face.

Lady Macduff's jaw hung open, a scream striving to free itself from her broken soul, yet she made no sound.

Her son, for his part, said to her in a simple, calm voice, "He has killed me, Mother." His voice rose only slightly in pitch when he added his final words: "Run away, I pray you!"

And then the boy dropped where he stood, dead.

Lady Macduff found her scream at last. Her strongest impulse was to rush to her slain little boy, but other shouts continued to sound through the halls of her home, and she had other children who – God be kind and willing! – still needed her. So she feigned a forward step, and when the intruder grabbed at her, she rushed around him and toward the door, calling, "Murder!" over and over at the top of her lungs.

The two intruders, the two *murderers,* their blades at the ready, pursued.

PART FOUR

CHAPTER THREE

Macduff stood together with the former King Duncan's elder son, Malcolm, on the open grounds before the royal palace of King Edward of England. The determined Macduff had been forced to plea his case to one English official after another, over and over, before he had been allowed to get this close to Malcolm – Edward sympathized with the Scottish expatriate, indeed.

And now Malcolm looked as though he wished he had refused to see Macduff after all. Upon hearing his description of the state of Scotland, the young Prince-who-should-be-King appeared ill.

His voice reflecting as much, Malcolm said, "Let us seek out some desolate shade, and there weep our sad bosoms empty."

But Macduff answered with a firm shake of his head. "Let us rather hold fast the deadly sword, and like good men stand in defense of our downfallen birth land. Each new morning new widows howl, new orphans cry, new sorrows strike Heaven on the face, until it resounds as if it felt with Scotland and yelled out in sympathetic pain."

Malcolm turned an intense gaze upon Macduff. "What I *believe*, I'll wail; what I *know*, I'll believe; and what I can redress – as I shall find the time favorable – I *will.* What you have spoken, it may perchance be so. This tyrant – whose mere name blisters our tongues! – was once thought honest; you have loved him well. He has not touched you yet." He inspected Macduff up and down. "I am inexperienced, but you may discern something of him through *me,* and find the wisdom to offer up a weak poor innocent lamb to appease an angry god."

Macduff's posture stiffened. "I am not treacherous."

"But Macbeth *is.* A good and virtuous nature may acquiesce to a King's imperial charge."

The two men glared at one another for a very long, tense moment ... until Malcolm backed down.

"But I shall crave your pardon," he apologized. "My thoughts cannot transpose that which you *are* – angels are still bright, though Lucifer, the brightest, fell." He shook his head and released a saddened sigh. "Though all things foul seek to wear the appearance of grace ... yet grace must still look like itself."

Macduff heaved his own sigh, one of frustration. "I have lost my hopes of your cooperation."

Malcolm returned, "Perchance even there where I did find my doubts of your loyalties. Why, in that unprotected state, did you leave your wife and children – those precious inspirations, those strong knots of love – without farewell?" When he saw Macduff's face reddening, in anger or anguish, he hurried to add, "I pray you, do not let my suspicions be your dishonors, but mine own safeties. You may be rightly just, whatever *I* shall think."

But Macduff turned his back on Malcolm in antipathy, and – his fists clenched before him – called northward, "Bleed, bleed, poor country! Great tyrant, lay sure your basis, for goodness dares not check you; wear your wrongs, for the title is confirmed!" He spun back to Malcolm, his features warped into a bitter sneer. "Fare you well, 'Lord.' I would not be the villain that you think for the whole space that's in the tyrant's grasp, and the rich East to boot." With that, Macduff marched away.

"Be not offended!" Malcolm called after him, and Macduff halted, though he kept his back to the young man. "I speak not as in *absolute* distrust of you. I think our country sinks beneath the yoke; it weeps, it bleeds, and each new day a gash is added to her wounds."

With clear reluctance, Macduff turned to face Malcolm once more.

Malcolm continued, speaking carefully, "I think as well there would be hands uplifted in my right; and from here, gracious King Edward has offered me goodly thousands of troops. But ..." Malcolm's head sagged, though he kept it just high enough to keep a watchful eye upon Macduff. "... for all this, when I shall tread upon the tyrant's head, or wear it on my sword, my poor country shall yet have more vices than it had before, more suffering and in more sundry ways than ever ... by him that shall succeed."

Curious, but still leery, Macduff approached Malcolm once more. "Who should he be?"

Breathing deeply, Malcolm stated, "It is *myself* I mean; in whom I know all the particulars of vice are so grafted that, when they shall be opened to the public, black Macbeth will seem as pure as snow, and the poor state of Scotland will esteem him as a lamb, being compared with *my* boundless harms."

Macduff scoffed, "Not in the legions of horrid Hell can come a devil more damned in evils to top Macbeth."

"I grant him bloody, lecherous, avaricious, false, deceitful, violent, malicious – smacking of every sin that has a name. But ..." Again, Malcolm's head sagged, this time in clear shame. "... there's no bottom, none, in *my* sexual desires."

Macduff was taken aback; whatever faults Malcolm might have revealed at this juncture, he had not expected this.

Malcolm elaborated, "Your wives, your daughters, your matrons, *and* your maids could not fill up the cistern of my lust, and my desire would overbear all restraining impediments that did oppose my will." The young man moaned under his breath before adding, "Better Macbeth than such a one to reign."

Drawing a deep breath, Macduff spoke in a cautious, delicate voice, "Boundless intemperance in a man's nature is a tyranny itself; it has been the untimely emptying of the happy throne, and fall of many Kings." In a show of support that surprised even himself, he touched the young man's arm. "But fear not yet to take upon you what is yours. You may manage, secretly, your pleasures in a spacious plenty, and yet *seem* chaste – the time you may so hoodwink." He cleared his throat, before continuing, "We have willing dames enough; there cannot be *that* vulture in you to devour so many as will dedicate themselves to greatness, if finding it so inclined."

But Malcolm shook his head. "Along with this, in my most ill-composed disposition, there grows such an insatiable avarice that – were I King – I should cut off the nobles for their lands, desire this one's jewels and this other's house; and my more-having would be as a sauce to make me hunger for *more,* that I should forge unjust quarrels against the good and loyal, destroying them for wealth."

This stopped Macduff short, at first. "This avarice

sticks deeper," he admitted, "grows with more pernicious root than youthful-seeming lust, and it has been the sword against our slain Kings." Then he rallied, "But do not fear; Scotland has abundant wealth – to which the King would be entitled – to fill up your will." Macduff offered him a forced smile. "All these weaknesses are bearable, when weighed against other graces."

Malcolm stepped back, away from Macduff's heartening hand. "But I have none. The King-becoming graces, such as justice, verity, temperance, stableness, bounty, perseverance, mercy, humility, devotion, patience, courage, fortitude ..." He shook his head. "I have no trace of them, but abound in the variations of each separate sin, acting it many ways." He thought for a moment, then shook his head again, firmer this time. "Nay, had I power, I should pour the sweet milk of harmony into Hell, tumult the universal peace, destroy all unity on Earth."

Macduff glared at the man in incredulity, and decried himself for having ever imagined finding salvation for his country in this despicable boy. "Oh, Scotland," he muttered, heartsick, "Scotland!"

"If such a one be fit to govern," Malcolm concluded in a soft voice, "speak. I am as I have spoken."

" 'Fit to govern'!" Macduff sputtered in bitter disbelief. "No, not to *live*." He faced northward once more. "Oh, miserable nation, with an untitled tyrant bloody-sceptered, when shall you see your wholesome days again, since the truest inheritor of your throne – by his own interdiction – stands accursed, and does defame his own breed?" Then he whirled back to Malcolm. "Your royal father was a most sainted King; the Queen that bore you, more often praying upon her knees than standing on her feet, was prepared for the afterlife every day she lived." Taking a cue from Malcolm's own previous behavior, he made a show of looking the young man up and down, and found what he inspected sorely lacking. "Fare you well! These evils you reported upon yourself have banished me from Scotland. Oh my breast, your hope ends here!"

But before Macduff could march away once more – for good this time – Malcolm rushed forward and seized the man by the arm with a desperate grasp. "Macduff—!"

Macduff glowered down at the offending hand, then up into Malcolm's face.

Wisely, Malcolm released his hold, but pursued his attention. "This noble passion, child of integrity, has wiped the black scruples from my soul, and reconciled my thoughts to your good truth and honor." He stood taller and with more confidence than when Macduff had first approached him. "Devilish Macbeth, by many of these stratagems, has sought to win me into his power, and modest wisdom blocks me from overcredulous haste, but may God above deal between you and me! For even now I put myself to your direction, and unspeak my own detraction, here recant the taints and blames I laid upon myself, as being strangers to my nature." Malcolm blushed and offered a self-conscious smile. "I am ... yet *unknown* to woman, never was forsworn, scarcely have coveted what was mine own, at no time broke my faith, would not betray the devil to his fellow, and delight no less in truth than life – my *first* false speaking was this upon myself."

Malcolm paused, gauging Macduff's reaction to this, his authentic confession. When he found the older man neither astounded nor accepting, but maintaining a rigidly neutral bearing, he continued.

"What I am truly," he stated with all strength and

sincerity, "is yours and my poor country's to command: Whither indeed, before you're here-approach, Old Siward – the English General, and mine own uncle – was setting forth with ten thousand warlike men, already prepared." It was Malcolm's turn to place a supportive hand upon Macduff's arm; Macduff tensed, but did not resist the touch. "Now we'll stand *together*, and may the chance of goodness be as strong as our quarrel is just!" When Macduff still did not respond, but held his clinical detachment, Malcolm implored, "Why are you silent?"

Unlike his countenance, Macduff could not keep his frustrated confusion from his voice. "Such welcome and *un*welcome things at once ... it is hard to reconcile."

Malcolm opened his mouth to reply, to reiterate that his "*un*welcome" presentation had been a ruse to test Macduff's principles, but when he spied an elderly doctor approaching from the English palace, he instead said, "Well, more later." He called to the doctor as the man drew nearer, "Comes the King forth, I pray you?"

The old man was startled at first, apparently having approached the Scotsmen by happenstance rather than intention. He blinked, seemed to recognize Malcolm, and replied, "Aye, sir; there are a crew of wretched souls that await his cure." The doctor shook his head. "Their malady confounds the greatest medical arts, but at his touch – such sanctity Heaven has given his hand! – they immediately amend."

Malcolm nodded. "I thank you, doctor."

The old doctor bowed his head to Malcolm, then to Macduff, and continued on his way.

"What's the disease he means?" Macduff asked.

"It is called scrofula, 'the evil': A most miraculous work in this good King Edward, which I have seen him do often since my here-remain in England. How he solicits Heaven, himself best knows; but strangely-afflicted people, all swollen and ulcerous, pitiful to the eye, the utter despair of surgery ... he *cures*, hanging a golden stamped coin about their necks, put on with holy prayers – and, it is spoken, he leaves the healing benediction to the succeeding royalty." Malcolm shook his head in wonder. "And with this strange power, he has a Heavenly gift of prophecy, and assorted blessings hang about his throne that speak him full of God's grace." [4]

Before Macduff could inquire further about these blessed abilities, they were again interrupted by the sight of an approaching figure; a visitor who, unlike the doctor, had to pass through the sentries before striking out across the palace grounds.

Macduff gestured toward the newcomer. "See who comes here."

"My countryman," Malcolm observed from the approaching man's clothing, "but yet I do not recognize him."

But as the man drew near, Macduff identified him at last, and was surprised to see Ross here. He called out, "My ever-noble cousin, welcome to this place."

---

[4]

Some scholars question the purpose of the doctor's appearance and the discussion of "the evil" that follows. While this is not viewed as material foreign to the original script, it has been noted that this brief sequence adds nothing to the plot – King Edward never appears; the disease never comes into play. They suggest this was possibly Shakespeare's pandering to the attending royals in his audience, particularly King James, who, as Edward's successor, would therefore have inherited this "healing benediction."

This prompted a nod of recognition from Malcolm; Ross had lost a noticeable amount of weight since Malcolm had last laid eyes upon him. "I know him now," he said as he raised a hand in greeting. "Good God, soon remove the condition that makes us strangers!"

As Ross reached them and shook their hands, he agreed, "Sir, amen."

"Stands Scotland where it did?" asked Macduff.

Ross moaned, "Alas, poor country! Almost afraid to know itself. It cannot be called our motherland, but our *grave*; where no one, but he who knows nothing, is once seen to smile; where sighs and groans and shrieks that rend the air are made, but not noticed; where violent sorrow seems a commonplace frenzy. The dead man's funeral bell there is scarcely asked for whom it rings, and good men's lives expire before the flowers in their caps wilt, dying before they sicken."

"Oh, this report!" Macduff spat. "Too precise, yet too true."

Malcolm, who had fled Scotland when this horror was still young, asked Ross, "What's the newest grief?"

"That of an hour's age does draw hisses at the speaker; each minute breeds a new one."

Macduff nodded his agreement with this assessment, once more facing north. He asked Ross, "How is my wife?"

"Why ... well."

Perhaps it was because Macduff was looking away that he did not notice Ross' hesitation, but Malcolm did.

"And all my children?"

"Well, too."

Malcolm observed how Ross shifted in discomfort upon this further report, how he looked to the ground even though Macduff could not return his gaze.

"The tyrant has not battered at their peace?"

"No, they ... were well at peace when I did leave 'em."

This exchange skewered Ross' composure most of all; Malcolm could see that he was choosing his words with excessive care, hedging the truth in some critical way – if not lying outright.

This did not bode well.

Macduff, too, finally detected that something was amiss. He turned to face Ross and said, "Be not stingy with your speech; how goes it?"

Ross grew expansive in a sudden – and, to Malcolm, suspicious – rush. "When I came here to transport the tidings, which I have heavily borne, there ran a rumor of many worthy fellows that were out in arms – which was to my belief made credible, for that I saw the tyrant's forces afoot." He addressed Malcolm, "Now is the time for your help; your eye in Scotland would create soldiers, make even our women fight, to shed their dire distresses."

With an affirming glance toward Macduff, Malcolm announced, "Let it be their comfort – we *are* coming there. Gracious King Edward has lent us good Siward and ten thousand men; Christendom proclaims no more experienced or better soldier."

Ross tried to smile, but his eyes shifted over to Macduff ... and he instead exhaled a woeful murmur. "If only I could answer this comfort with the like! But I have words that demand to be howled out in the deserted air, where hearing should not catch them."

"Whom do they concern?" Macduff asked, though Malcolm noticed that he had already stiffened. "The general cause? Or is it a private grief, belonging to some single breast?"

"No mind that's honest could help but share some woe ..." Ross answered, his eyes downcast, "... though the main part pertains to you alone."

Macduff's spine now tightened like tempered steel. "If it be mine," he whispered, "keep it not from me. *Quickly* let me have it."

But still Ross stalled. "Do not let your ears despise my tongue forever," he begged, his discomfort excruciating to witness, "which shall possess them with the heaviest sound that they ever yet heard."

Malcolm expected Macduff to seize the man – uncomfortable or not, Ross was selfish to drag this out so painfully!

Instead, Macduff hunched over, making a strangled "Humh!" sound as though he might vomit. His eyes tearing up and haunted, as downcast as Ross' own, he gasped, "I guess at it ..."

Finally, Ross divulged the terrible news. "Your castle was surprised; your wife and babes savagely ... slaughtered. To relate the manner would add the death of *you* onto the mound of corpses of these murdered deer."

"Merciful Heaven!" Malcolm cried.

Macduff collapsed to his knees, his hands covering his face as he lamented in total silence.

Malcolm knelt beside him and tried to pull his hands away. "What, man! Never hide your heartache! Give sorrow *words*. The grief that does not speak whispers to the overburdened heart and bids it *break*."

Macduff allowed Malcolm to lower his arms, but his wet eyes sought Ross. "My *children*, too?"

Ross, his own cheeks moist, nodded. "Wife, children, servants ... all that could be found."

"And I must be *from* there!" Macduff raged at himself, clenching his fists as though he intended to strike his own face. But he just as quickly deflated again, asking in senseless desperation. "My *wife* killed, too?"

Ross' face reddened beyond sadness to resentment at being forced to repeat these horrid words over and over, but he managed to keep his voice flat as he stated, "I have said."

This time Macduff groaned audibly and collapsed sideways, but Malcolm was there to catch him. He held the weeping man in his arms and said, "Be comforted. Let's make us medicines of our great revenge, to cure this deadly grief."

Without warning, Macduff shoved Malcolm away and rose to his feet. Looming over him, Macduff cried, "*Macbeth* has no children!" He whirled toward Ross and demanded, "*All* my pretty ones? Did you say *all*?"

Ross nodded.

"Oh, Hell-bird! *All?* What, *all* my pretty chickens and their mother in one fell swoop?!"

Helpless, Ross nodded once more.

Malcolm stood. "Contest it like a man."

"I shall do so," Macduff swore through clenched teeth, with new fire in his voice, "but I must also *feel* it as a man: I cannot help but remember how such things were, that were most precious to me. Did Heaven look on this slaughter, and would not help them?" He shook his head, his gaze turned inward. "Sinful Macduff, they were all struck on account of *you*! Wicked man that *I* am, not for their own demerits, but for *mine*, slaughter fell on their souls. Heaven rest them now!"

"Let this be the whetstone of your sword," Malcolm urged, "let grief convert to anger; blunt not the heart, *enrage* it."

Macduff glared at Malcolm, but he nodded. "Oh, I could play the woman with mine eyes and braggart with my tongue! But, gentle Heavens, cut short all delay. You bring face-to-face this fiend of Scotland and myself, set him within my sword's length ..." Macduff fairly growled, "... if he escapes, may Heaven forgive him, too!"

Malcolm nodded in satisfaction. "*This* tune goes manly. Come, we'll go to the King; our army is ready, our only lack is his royal leave." He shook his fist. "Macbeth is ripe for shaking, and the powers above arm themselves. Receive what cheer you may, the night is long that never finds the day."

PART FIVE

CHAPTER ONE

Heavy night enveloped the castle in Dunsinane, where King Macbeth had recently relocated his throne. Shadows flickered about the anteroom beyond the new bedchambers of the Queen, Lady Macbeth. A large fireplace was the primary source of warmth and light at this time of night, though a large number of candles still burned here and there around the anteroom and the short hallway leading to where the Queen slept.

The Doctor of Physic waited in the farthest corner from the fireplace, and a constant chill threatened to shiver its way into his old bones. The Queen's waiting-gentlewoman, a lady greater than his own age, appeared equally uncomfortable in this relentless cold, but she had steadfastly insisted they wait here in this darkened nook.

The doctor, however, was beginning to feel that enough was enough.

"Two nights I have watched with you," he said in a low voice, "but can perceive no truth in your report." He rubbed his hands over his crossed arms, as much to warm himself as to make sure she understood his duress. "When was it she last walked?"

"Since His Majesty went into the field of battle," she replied in a quivering voice, "I have seen her rise from her bed, throw her nightgown upon her, unlock her closet, take forth paper, fold it, write upon it, read it, afterwards seal it, and again return to bed – yet all this while in a most fast sleep."

The doctor grunted his disapproval. "A great disturbance in nature, to receive at once the benefit of sleep, and do the actions of one awake!" He considered a moment, then asked, "In this slumbery agitation – besides her walking and other actual performances – what, at any time, have you heard her say?"

The gentlewoman sniffed. "That, sir, which I will *not* report after her."

The doctor was taken aback. "You may to me, and it is most fitting you should."

"Neither to you nor anyone," she insisted, "having no witness to *confirm* my speech." The doctor opened his mouth to redress her further, but she then spotted a new light twinkling in the hallway to the Queen's bedchamber. "Look you, here she comes!"

The Queen entered, her nightgown slung idly over her shoulders – the doctor was aghast to see the front remained open, exposing her breasts and pubis for anyone to see! She strode with a sluggish step through the anteroom, a thin taper candle held before her, the melted wax flowing down over the flesh of her hand without her seeming to notice.

"This is her very guise," the gentlewoman explained, "and, upon my life, fast asleep. Observe her, but stand out of sight."

"How did she come by that light?"

"Why, it stood by her bed. She has light by her continually; it is her command."

The doctor noted that the Queen shuffled across the anteroom without colliding with any of the furniture. "You see, her eyes are open."

"Aye, but their sense is shut."

The Queen had reached a cabinet upon which rested a large basin. With a clumsy effort, she placed her taper into an awaiting candlestick, and though the basin was currently empty of water, she reached into it as though she were washing.

"What is it she does now?" the doctor asked in confusion. "Look how she rubs her hands."

"It is an accustomed action with her," the gentlewoman explained, "to seem thus washing her hands. I have known her to continue in this a quarter of an hour."

Then, to the doctor's surprise and the gentlewoman's unease, the Queen began to mumble. "Yet here's a spot ..." she said as she scrubbed at the back of one hand.

"Hark," the doctor whispered, "she speaks!" He scrambled to produce a small slate and some chalk from his robes, his cold hands slow to cooperate. "I will set down what comes from her, to confirm my remembrance the more strongly."

The Queen grew upset, both with her hand-scrubbing and in her voice. "Out, damned spot! *Out*, I say! One ... two ..." She looked toward them; for a moment, the doctor thought she had finally noticed them, but the gentlewoman knew better. "Why then, it is time to do it." She cast around her. "Hell is murky ..." Back toward them, but certainly not *to* them. "Fie, my Lord, fie! A soldier, and afraid? What need *we* fear who knows it, when none can call our power to account?" And slowly, her gaze was drawn back toward her hands. "Yet ... who would have thought the old man to have had *so much* blood in him ..."

The doctor gasped. "Do you mark that?" he rasped

to the gentlewoman, who only nodded.

"The Thane of Fife had a wife," the Queen keened, "where is *she* now?" She scrubbed her hands in such fierceness and desperation, the doctor feared she might rip open her flesh. But the tears upon the Queen's cheek did not reflect physical pain. "What, will these hands *never* be clean?" She spun around, facing the nothing behind her. "No more of that, my Lord," she scolded, "no more of that; you mar all with this startled behavior."

"Come, come," the doctor muttered to the gentlewoman, "you have heard what you should not."

The gentlewoman countered, "She has *spoke* what she should not, I am sure of that. Heaven knows what she has known."

Lady Macbeth was facing the basin once more. "Here's the smell of the blood still," she moaned as she scrubbed herself raw. "All the perfumes of Arabia will not sweeten this little hand." She scoured harder at the imagined blood stains. "Oh, oh, *oh*!"

"What a sigh is there!" the doctor commented in pity. "The heart is sorely burdened."

The gentlewoman agreed, "I would not have such a heart in my bosom for the worth of the whole body."

The doctor watched the Queen a moment longer, then said in resignation, "Well, well, well."

"Pray to God it *be* well, sir."

"This disease is beyond my skills; but I have known those which have walked in their sleep who have died piously in their beds."

The Queen interrupted them as she whirled around again. "Wash your hands, put on your nightgown, do not look so pale." She shook her head at whatever she heard the silence say. "I tell you yet again, Banquo's *buried*; he cannot come out of his grave."

Even more? the doctor marveled.

Lady Macbeth's frenzy grew. "To bed, to bed!" She seized her taper and ushered her unseen – but certainly not un*known*, at least to the doctor's perception – partner in crime back toward her bedchamber. "There's knocking at the gate. Come, come, *come, come!* Give me your hand. What's done cannot be *un*done. To bed, to bed, to bed ..."

And with that, the Queen retreated from sight.

"Will she go now to bed?" the doctor asked.

"Directly."

The doctor considered the perverse scene they had just witnessed. "Foul whisperings are abroad. Unnatural deeds do breed unnatural troubles; infected minds will discharge, to their deaf pillows, their secrets." He shook his head. "She more needs the *divine* than the physician. God, God forgive us all!" He took the gentlewoman's hand in earnest. "Look after her, remove from her all the means of self-injury, and constantly keep eyes upon her." He paused, but what more was there to say on this dark matter? "So, goodnight. She has confused my mind, and amazed my sight. I think ... but dare not speak."

The gentlewoman squeezed the doctor's hand in understanding, and gratitude that she no longer bore this heavy knowledge alone. "Good night, good Doctor."

They parted ways.

Part Five

Chapter Two

In the countryside near Dunsinane, a drum beat as a merging of marshal colors took place – of English advance scouts and Scottish rebel forces. Those who were more often tense allies, if not outright enemies, shook glad hands with one another, for they stood united in their causes against the tyranny of the "King," Macbeth.

On a hillside near the northern perimeter of the temporary camp, one group of insurgent Scottish nobles huddled close together as they overlooked the gathering below.

"The English power is near," said Menteth, "led on by Malcolm, his uncle Siward, and the good Macduff. Revenges burn in them; for their heartfelt causes would excite even the dead man to the bleeding and the grim call of battle."

Angus agreed. "We shall no doubt meet them near Birnam wood; they are coming that way."

Cathness asked the others, "Who knows if Donalbain is with his brother?" Unlike Malcolm, almost nothing had been heard of the younger Prince since he fled to Ireland.

"For certain, sir," Lennox answered with a shake of his head, "he is *not.* I have a list of all the nobility. There is Siward's son, and many unbearded youths that even now proclaim their first of manhood."

"What of the tyrant?" Menteth asked.

Cathness answered with distaste, "He strongly fortifies great Dunsinane. Some say he's mad; others, that hate him less, do call it 'valiant fury.' But, for certain, he cannot buckle his diseased cause within the belt of self-control."

With obvious pleasure, Angus added, "Now he does feel the blood of his secret murders sticking on his hands. Now minutely revolts reproach his faith-breach; those he commands move *only* in command, not for love. *Now* he does feel his title hang loose about him, like a giant's robe upon a dwarfish thief."

"Who then shall blame his troubled senses to recoil and start," Menteth mused, "when all that is within him does condemn itself for being there?"

Cathness looked further outward, spying the first signs of the core forces from England as they neared the wood of Birnam. "Well, *we* march on to give obedience where it is truly owed. We meet Malcolm, the medicine of the sickly state, and with him we pour each drop of our blood in our country's purge."

Lennox seconded, "Or so much blood as it needs to water the sovereign flower and drown the weeds." He offered a bold gesture. "We make our march towards Birnam!"

Together, the Scottish noblemen advanced.

PART FIVE

CHAPTER THREE

In the war counsel chamber of the King's new castle at Dunsinane, parchment crackled as Macbeth crumpled it into his fist. Four pages thick it was – the latest lists of Scottish Thanes who had publicly disavowed their sacred oaths to the throne. Flakes of parchment wafted down onto the map- and report-laden table where the King sat.

The attendants, who all stood opposite the King, waited in dreaded patience for the outburst they knew would come. They had learned to recognize the manic gleam in their monarch's eye, and their predictions were correct.

Macbeth hurled the pages at the hobbled young man who had brought them. "Bring me no more reports!" he bellowed. "Let them all fly! Till Birnam wood moves to Dunsinane, *I* cannot be tainted with fear!"

The messenger bowed and limped gratefully away, out of the room and as far as possible from the King's wrath. The other attendants were not so lucky; indeed, the doctor – who had come to report his latest evaluation of the Queen – hung back among them, hoping that perhaps his sovereign might forget about him altogether.

"What's the boy Malcolm?" Macbeth demanded of the room at large. "Was he not born of woman? The spirits that know all mortal destinies have pronounced me thus: 'Fear not, Macbeth, no man that's born of woman shall ever have power upon thee.' " His grin that followed chilled the doctor's heart. "Then *fly*, false Thanes, and mingle with the English decadents! The mind I rule by and the heart I bear shall never sag with doubt nor shake with fear."

The chamber door opened once more, admitting a servant boy, one even younger than the messenger before him but surer of foot. Not that any of this meant anything to the irate King.

"The Devil damn you black, you cream-faced loon!" the King snapped. "Where did you get that goose look?"

The servant swallowed hard, and croaked, "There is ten thousand—"

"Geese, villain?" Macbeth mocked.

"Soldiers, sir."

Macbeth's derisive smile faded into a snarl. "Go prick your face, and over-redden your fear, you lily-livered boy. *What* soldiers, fool?" When the messenger did not immediately answer, the King jammed a finger toward the boy's face, prompting him to flinch. "Death on your soul! Those linen cheeks of yours are advocates of fear. *What soldiers*, whey-face?!"

"The English force ... so please you."

Macbeth fell motionless, his countenance even darker than before, prompting the messenger – and others behind him – to question whether he would leave this room alive. Indeed, the King's hand drifted toward an ornate dagger he had the habit of carrying with him about the castle ...

... but in the end, he merely gestured toward the door and grumbled, "Take your face hence."

The servant retreated posthaste, exiting in such a hurry that he left the chamber door open behind him.

Macbeth remained still, however, and brooded. His attendants and the doctor waited in absolute silence.

Without warning, Macbeth rose and barked, "Seyton!" toward the open doorway. He paced on his side of the table. The others continued to hold their place.

I am sick at heart, Macbeth thought, *when I behold—*

He interrupted his own reflections when he realized that his officer had not instantly appeared. "Seyton, I say!" he roared. His focus then returned inward.

This crisis will cheer me ever or dethrone me now. I have lived long enough: My course of life is fallen into the autumn, like the yellow leaf, and that which should accompany old age – such as honor, love, obedience, troops of friends – I must not look to have; but in their stead, curses, *not loud but deep, mouth-honor, and* breath, *which the poor heart would gladly deny ... and dare not.*

Macbeth sighed, and then realized that Seyton still had not shown himself. "*Seyton!*" he raged.

At last, and to the relief of all, Seyton rushed through the doorway, sweat upon his brow and breathing heavy from a run. "What is your gracious pleasure?" he asked the King with a bow.

For his part, Macbeth behaved as if there had been no delay at all. "What more news?"

"All is confirmed, my Lord, which was reported."

Macbeth mulled this over, then nodded in decision. "I'll fight till my flesh be hacked from my bones. Give me my armor."

"It is not needed yet," Seyton assured him.

"I'll put it on," Macbeth insisted. "Send out more horses, scour the country round; *hang* those that talk of fear." He then repeated, his words clear and cold. "Give me my armor."

Seyton bowed his head and snapped his fingers at the attendants. The room broke into hushed pandemonium as they hurried to assemble the King's armor and dress him. This also served to better reveal the doctor's presence, and to the old man's regret, Macbeth finally noticed him.

The King asked about his wife, "How is your patient, Doctor?"

Choosing his words carefully, the doctor replied, "Not so sick, my Lord, as she is troubled with thick-coming fancies that keep her from her rest."

"Cure her of that," Macbeth commanded as his breastplate was placed upon him. "Can you not minister to a diseased *mind* – pluck a rooted sorrow from the memory, wipe out the troubles written on the brain and, with some sweet forgetful antidote, cleanse the stuffed bosom of that perilous stuff which weighs upon the heart?"

The doctor licked his lips. "Therein the patient must minister to herself."

Macbeth seized the gauntlet that a servant was about to place upon his hand and threw it at the doctor; the old man barely ducked in time. "Throw medicine to the dogs, I'll none of it!"

The doctor dropped his humble gaze to the floor as he bowed.

"Come, put my armor on," Macbeth groused – dismissing, of course, that it was his own action that caused the latest delay. "Give me my lance. Seyton, send out the soldiers."

Seyton nodded, placing upon the table the sheathed sword which he had been about to strap onto the King's side, and clapped his hands toward a Lieutenant waiting just outside the chamber.

"Doctor," Macbeth began, "the Thanes fly from me— Come, sir, dispatch!"

Seyton realized the King was addressing him once more, and hurried to reclaim Macbeth's sword.

Macbeth continued, "If you could, Doctor, examine the urine of my land, find her disease, and purge it to a sound and pristine health, I would applaud you to the very echo, that should applaud again." He was again distracted as some dullard attempted to place a royal cloak upon the shoulders of his armor. What fool saw this as proper battle attire? "Pull it off, I say!" Returning his attention to the doctor, he asked, "What rhubarb plant, flower, or what purgative drug, would scour these English from this place? Have you heard of them?"

Cowed more than ever, the doctor offered, "Aye, my good Lord; *your* royal preparation makes us hear something."

Macbeth chuckled, an unpleasant sound. The doctor held his breath ...

At last, the King turned away from the doctor and gestured toward the remainder of his armor. "Bring it after me," he pronounced to his entourage. "*I* will not be afraid of death and bane, till Birnam forest come to Dunsinane."

King Macbeth marched out of the war chamber, Seyton and his attendants chasing after him with assorted bits of armor and weaponry.

The doctor released such a sigh of relief that he felt dizzy. Leaning against the cluttered table, he rubbed a shaking hand over his sweaty face.

Were I away and clear from Dunsinane, no profit should hardly draw me here again.

CHAPTER FOUR

The English army and Scottish mutineers came together in full force. Drums echoed through the hills around them, the Scottish nobles who led the insurgency marched under the flags of truce, lest they suffer some fatal misunderstanding as they sought and found their true liege, Prince Malcolm – *King* Malcolm, if their cause triumphed.

"Cousins," Malcolm greeted them with ample warmth, "I hope the days are near at hand that sleeping chambers will be safe."

Menteth shook the Prince's hand with vigor even as he bowed his head. "We doubt it nothing."

The great English warrior, Malcolm's Uncle Siward, stepped forward and nodded his head toward the nearby forest. "What wood is this before us?"

"The wood of Birnam," Menteth replied.

Malcolm's eyes brightened as providence struck him. "Let every soldier hew down a bough and bear it before him," he commanded the nearest officer, "thereby shall we conceal the numbers of our host and make reconnaissance err in report of us."

"It shall be done," the soldier promised as he hurried off to relay Malcolm's orders.

Siward mulled over this idea before smiling his

approval. He commented, "We learn nothing else but that the confident tyrant remains still in Dunsinane, and will endure our laying siege to it."

Malcolm nodded. "It is his main hope; for where there is opportunity to be given, both the great and lowly have given him the revolt, and none serve with him but those constrained, whose hearts are absent, too."

Macduff, who had brooded in dark silence through most of their advance, spoke up. "Let our just censures await the true outcome, and we put on industrious soldiership."

Siward agreed. "The time approaches that will, with due decision, make us know what we shall *say* we have and what we *truly* own. Speculative thoughts relate their unsure hopes, but certain issue *battles* must arbitrate." He then raised his voice for all to hear, calling out at the top of his lungs, "Towards which ... *advance the war!*"

Scottish soldiers and English alike echoed his cry and, now cloaked behind a deceptive facade of Birnam wood, they marched onward.

Part Five

Chapter Five

As the afternoon stretched out toward dusk, the castle at Dunsinane bustled with activity, Macbeth's remaining forces preparing for the coming siege. Drums played and flags waved, every bit as loud and audacious as those of the advancing enemy – the King made sure of that.

"Hang out our banners on the outward walls," Macbeth commanded in raucous bluster as he entered the courtyard, "the cry is still 'They come!' Our castle's strength will laugh a siege to scorn!" He, too, laughed, a harsh bark that startled Seyton and his attendants. "Let them lie here till famine and fever eat them up! Were they not reinforced with those that should be *ours*, we might have met them boldly, beard to beard, and beat them backward home!"

Macbeth tossed an expectant glance over his shoulder, and his attendants hurried to cheer for the King's courageous proclamations. For if Macbeth said it, it must be so – they had learned this lesson well.

Macbeth continued his traipse across the courtyard when a shrill cry suddenly echoed from the opposite end of the yard. The first voice was almost immediately joined by another, and another still. The King craned his neck, but with all the flurrying movement in the way, he could see nothing, could not ascertain its exact location or cause.

"What is that noise?" he snapped to anyone and no one in particular. He did not care for the interruption.

"It is the cry of women, my good Lord," Seyton replied. And when Macbeth clapped his hands, Seyton bowed and rushed across the yard to investigate.

I have almost forgot the taste of fears, Macbeth mused as he waited. *The time has been, my senses would have cooled to hear a night-shriek; and the hair on my skin would, at a dismal treatise, rouse and stir as if life were in it.* He smirked with some facsimile of pride. *I have supped full with horrors; direness, familiar to my slaughterous thoughts, cannot ever startle me.*

Then Seyton was returning, and Macbeth recognized a dismal dread upon the man's face. It irritated him; with such threats from without, what news could be so bad from within?

"For what was that cry?" he demanded.

Seyton tried to speak, cleared his throat, then stated, "The Queen, my Lord ... is dead."

All eyes turned toward the King.

Macbeth stood silent, at first. How should he react to this most terrible news? He did not know. He sought the truth of his feelings deep within his heart, but all he found was murk and confusion. Pain? Perhaps. But such pain would have to be born of love ... and like fear, love had become something of a stranger to him of late.

A path cleared, as his subjects expected him to rush to her, to see his wife's death with his own eyes. But that very opening was enough for him to make out her broken body upon the courtyard ground – she had jumped from the tower above; had he not been swept up in his proclamations of superiority over his enemies, he might have seen her fall. He felt no desire for a closer inspection.

Macbeth remained where he stood.

She would have died hereafter, he told himself as he stared at the lonely shape across from him. *There would have been* some *time for such news. Tomorrow ... and tomorrow ... and tomorrow ... creeps in this petty pace from day to day, to the last syllable of recorded time, and all our yesterdays have lighted the way to dusty death for all fools.* He closed his eyes for a moment, his only outward sign of any feeling for this tragedy. *Out, out, brief candle! Life's nothing but a walking shadow, a poor player that struts and frets his hour upon the stage, and then is heard no more. It is a tale told by an idiot, full of sound and fury, signifying* nothing.

When Macbeth opened his eyes again, he found a panting, forlorn messenger before him – one who, judging by the ranking upon his sleeve, had run all the way down from his station at the highest hillside to report something, and who now, standing before his King, had lost the power of speech.

"You come to use your tongue," Macbeth stated with detached annoyance. "Your story, quickly."

The messenger – yet another too-young lad, for who else remained loyal to their King but those too young, too old, or too decrepit to betray him? – struggled to do as he was commanded. "My gracious Lord ... I should report that which I say I saw ... but do not know how to do it ..."

Macbeth's irritation grew. "Well, *say*, sir."

The lad nodded and stuttered, "As I did stand my watch upon the hill ... I looked toward Birnam, and at once I *thought* ..." He swallowed and shook his head, as though he doubted his memory now as he must have questioned his eyes then. "The wood began to *move*."

In a lightning flash that startled everyone, including Macbeth himself, the King drew his sword and held the point at the messenger's throat. "Liar and slave!" he roared.

The messenger squeezed his eyes shut in terror, tears already streaming down his face, but he stood his ground – literally as well as figuratively. "Let me endure your wrath, if it be not so!" He pointed a shaking hand toward the forest. "Within these three miles you may see it coming; I say ... *a moving grove.*"

"If you speak false," Macbeth hissed, his teeth so clenched his words were thick, "you shall hang alive upon the next tree, till famine wither you." Then, in a whisper so soft those around him could barely hear, he added, "If your speech be *truth* ... I do not care if you do as much for *me.*"

If this which he avouches does appear ...

Macbeth glared at the boy a moment longer, then dashed toward the nearest staircase to the castle platform, Seyton and his attendants scrambling to chase after him. Between his years at Inverness and time upon the throne at Forres, he was not nearly as familiar with the castle here at Dunsinane, and in his haste he nearly lost his way...

And when he at last stood amongst the scattered sentries atop the platform, he almost wished that he had.

The messenger had spoken the truth after all. Fear, which he had been mocking just minutes ago, seized his heart in its icy grip as, across the entire hillside, the woods of Birnam appeared to be shambling toward them.

He knew this could not literally be the case, of course. His strategic mind grasped in an instant what Malcolm's forces were doing. A wise move; worthy of his own battle experience.

But the *symbology* of it ...

Damn the Weïrd Sisters to Hell!

I reign in my confidence, and begin to doubt the equivocation of the fiend *that lies like truth. "Fear not, till Birnam wood do come to Dunsinane" ... and now a wood comes toward Dunsinane.*

He gaped at the approaching tree line a moment longer, and then his pale face tightened once more into a snarl of indomitability.

"To arms!" he bellowed. "To arms, and march out!"

His lingering subjects hurried to make it so.

There is neither flying away nor tarrying here. I begin to be weary of the sun, and wish the order of the world were now undone.

"Ring the alarm-bell!" he roared, raising his sword high, then pointing it in defiance toward the approaching Birnam wood. "Blow, wind! Come, ruin! At least we'll die with armor on our back."

Once again, Macbeth of Scotland prepared to wade headlong into battle.

Part Five

Chapter Six

Macbeth's conscripts emerged from the castle walls even as the English and rebel forces reached the plain before Dunsinane. The false-King's unexpected move made little sense to Siward or the others, as it created a vulnerability in their chances of braving the siege. With the castle so fortified, why would Macbeth choose to—?

So be it! If such a strategic blunder served to unseat the tyrant that much sooner, so much the better.

"Near enough now!" Malcolm called out from behind his camouflaging bough. "Throw down your leafy screens, and show yourselves like those you are!" He cast aside his own branch and said to Siward, "You, worthy Uncle, shall – with my cousin, your right-noble son – lead our first battalion. Worthy Macduff and we shall take upon us what else remains to do, according to our plan."

Siward bowed his head to the rightful King of Scotland and offered a fierce smile as he drew his sword. "Fare you well. If we do find the tyrant's power tonight, let us be *beaten*, if we cannot *fight*."

"Make all our trumpets speak!" Macduff cried with exuberance born of righteous rage. "Give them all breath, those clamorous harbingers of blood and death!"

The trumpets sang, and the opposing forces engaged...

PART FIVE

CHAPTER SEVEN

The battle proceeded poorly, far worse than Macbeth might have feared.

All around him, his remaining followers were *surrendering* to Malcolm's army more often than they fought back. The ungrateful, disloyal miscreants! He should have slaughtered them with his own sword, one and all!

Alarms sounded all around. Macbeth had barely taken to the field of combat himself before the castle was breached – if "breached" were the word for such a contemptible, one-sided fight. He withdrew, not bothering to call a formal retreat, for his degenerate "soldiers" were in complete disarray. And even as he reentered the main courtyard, he found that Malcolm's supporters had already circled around to the far side of Dunsinane and were invading from that end as well.

They have tied me to a stake, he realized, *I cannot fly, but, like a bear chained for sport, I must fight the full round.* He shook himself, angry at his moment of quivering. *Where's he that was not born of woman? Such a one am I to fear, or* none.

Macbeth rounded toward an access corridor that should have led him to the castle armory, but again, his comparatively short time in Dunsinane betrayed him, and he lost his way.

Forced to backtrack, he nearly collided with an English officer.

Macbeth and Siward's son stepped away from one another, each sizing the other up.

After a tense moment, Young Siward demanded, "What is your name?"

The bearer of the Scottish crown smiled. "You'll be afraid to hear it."

"No," Young Siward replied, hefting his sword between them, "though you call yourself a hotter name than any is in Hell."

Macbeth remained silent at first, still sizing up his opponent. Then, with pride, he stated, "My name's *Macbeth*."

Young Siward's eyes widened, though less in fear and more with excitement. "The Devil himself could not pronounce a title more hateful to my ear."

"No," Macbeth agreed, "nor more *fearful*."

Young Siward shook his head in firm denial. "You lie, abhorred tyrant; with my sword I'll prove the lie you speak!"

Young Siward had energy, as well as fresh training from a seasoned father on his side. But long before Macbeth ever heard the temptations of the three witches, he had fought his way to the rank of General, had turned the tide on repeated insurrections against King Duncan; he was a man feared long before he stole the crown.

They crossed swords, they pressed one another up and down the corridor a handful of times, they each drew the other's blood ... but, in the end, it was Young Siward who lain slain upon the castle floor.

Victorious, but still heaving for breath from the intense fight, Macbeth growled, with a smug sneer upon his face, "You were *born of woman*. Swords I smile at, weapons I laugh to scorn – brandished by any man that's of a woman born!"

Orienting himself once more, Macbeth made his way toward the armory. One or two more English soldiers entered from side doors as he proceeded, but he dispatched each of them in little time and with little interest ...

Out on the field of battle, a rage-driven Macduff pursued the few lingering sounds of combat.

The noise is that way.

"Tyrant, show your face!" Macduff screamed. "If you are slain and with no stroke of mine, my wife and children's ghosts will haunt me still!"

I cannot strike at wretched peasant soldiers, he thought, *whose arms are hired to bear their spears. Either* you, *Macbeth, or else I sheathe my sword again undeeded, with an unbattered edge.*

From within the castle's now-open gates, a surge of clashing blades reached out to his ears.

There *you should be!* Macduff grinned in dark satisfaction. *By this great clatter, one of greatest note seems announced. Let me find him, Fortune! And I beg not more.*

Even as Macduff hurried toward the newest crescendo of battle, he was met by Malcolm and Siward.

"This way, my Lord," Siward urged him on, "the castle's easily surrendered! The tyrant's people do fight on *both* sides, the noble Thanes do bravely in the war – the day almost professes itself yours, and little is left to do."

Malcolm shook his head in pleased disbelief. "We have met with foes that strike beside us rather than *at* us."

Siward gestured for Macduff to lead the way. "Enter, sir, the castle."

Somehow gripping his sword even tighter than before, Macduff hurled himself toward his promised justice.

Part Five

Chapter Eight [5]

All was lost. Macbeth could see that now. No more delusions.

His reign was over.

He emerged from the armory with a shield to accompany his sword, but nothing else. Why waste his time with a spear or helmet? Why drag this out any further? What was the point?

Indeed. What *was* the point?

As he stood in the corridor, Macbeth noted the lack of noise; no swords clashed, no cries echoed. The battle was over. The Prince of Chamberlain would become the King of Scotland after all.

No throne, no crown ... and no Lady Macbeth by his side.

It was all for *nothing*.

For a long, pronounced moment, Macbeth gazed down upon his sword, still wet with the blood of Young Siward and a few others. Why not add his own blood to the mix?

---

[5]

Some editions of *Macbeth* have this scene play through, unbroken, from the prior scene, rather than starting "Scene VIII."

He turned the sword edgewise, watching the torchlight gleam off its sharp metal. It would be so easy, so quick if his stroke was deep and swift ...

But in the end, he lowered the blade to his side.

Why should I play the ancient Roman fool, and die on my own sword? While I see living enemies, the gashes do better upon them.

As if on cue, a cold – yet, somehow, also heated – voice called from behind him. "Turn, Hell-hound, turn!"

Macbeth did so, and was not the least surprised to find Macduff glaring at him from the bend in the corridor, his sword and shield at the ready.

"Of all other men," Macbeth told him in a tired voice, "I have avoided *you*. But get back; my soul is too much charged with blood of yours already."

Rather than get back, Macduff advanced. "I have no words," he spat, "my voice is in my *sword*, you bloodier villain than words can label you!"

Macduff lunged, and Macbeth's instincts seized command.

They clashed repeatedly, Macduff fighting with less finesse than Young Siward before him, but a great deal more force. He was holding nothing back, paying no great attention to his own safety, only a burning desire to end Macbeth's life.

Twice Macbeth nearly slipped his blade through Macduff's sloppy defenses, but both times Macduff's shield did its duty. Then Macduff lunged too deeply in one thrust, allowing Macbeth to drag his sword across the weaker armor along his opponent's wrist; the cut was insufficient to disarm Macduff, but blood was drawn.

Eventually, their exchanges slowed as fatigue took its toll. Their swords continued to cross, but at a diminished pace.

"You lose your labor," Macbeth panted through a ruthless grin. "You may as easily impress the intangible *air* with your keen sword as make *me* bleed!" He laughed even as he parried Macduff's next attack. "Let your blade fall on vulnerable heads – *I* bear a charmed life, which must not yield to one born of woman."

To Macbeth's consternation, his words did not frighten Macduff, but somehow seemed to amuse the man. Macduff stood tall and proclaimed, "Despair of your 'charm,' and let the fallen angel whom you have still served tell you: *Macduff was prematurely ripped from his mother's womb!*"

Before Macduff's very eyes, the murdering devil who wore the Scottish crown dwindled from an arrogant, overconfident tyrant to a shaken, recreant shadow of his previous self.

"Accursed be that tongue that tells me so ..." Macbeth spoke in a raspy whisper, "... for it has cowed my manly valor!" He shook his head, his eyes drifting away from Macduff, staring at three sisters whom only he could see, "And let these beguiling *fiends* be no more believed, that equivocated with me in a double sense, that keep the word of promise to my ear ... and break it to my hope."

Macbeth looked to Macduff once more, and dropped his sword to the floor. Macduff gaped, both amazed and disgruntled.

Macbeth stated, "I'll not fight with you."

Outraged and thwarted – for how could he simply slaughter an unarmed man, however contemptible? What would the souls of his wife and children think of that? – Macduff demanded, "Then yield yourself, coward, and live to be the show and gaze of the time! We'll have you, as our rarer monsters are, with your painted likeness suspended upon a pole, and underwritten, '*Here* you may see *the tyrant!*' "

Macbeth gasped at the notion of being mocked like a freak, displayed before the public he had so recently held beneath his worthy heel. His eyes darkened, and gleamed with more than a little madness. Before Macduff could react, he stooped to retrieve his sword.

"I will *not* yield," Macbeth sputtered, foamy saliva spraying with his words, "to kiss the ground before young Malcolm's feet, and to be harassed by the rabble's curses. Though Birnam wood has come to Dunsinane ... and opposed by you, being of no woman born ... yet I will fight to the last." He shook his left arm until his shield came loose, then tossed it to the floor between them, both hands clutching the hilt of his sword. "Before my body I throw my warlike shield. Lay on, Macduff, and damned be him that first cries, 'Hold, enough!' "

Macduff nodded his wordless agreement, and the enemies engaged once more.

PART FIVE

CHAPTER NINE [6]

The battle won, Scotland was theirs.

Malcolm, Siward, several surviving Thanes, and many of the soldiers gathered together in the castle courtyard. An air of celebration surrounded Dunsinane; those who had remained "loyal" to Macbeth, only to surrender peacefully at the first opportunity, were allowed to join in.

But still they waited for final word on the fate of the tyrant. Numerous sentries were scattered around the castle grounds to ensure the tyrant could not escape, but for Malcolm, the fight was not truly over until Macbeth was in their hands – dead or alive.

"I wish the friends we miss were safely arrived," Malcolm stated as he took quiet count of those they had lost in the fight, and that count grew steadily with each report. It had been an easy victory, to be sure, when compared to how things might have gone if Macbeth had

------

6

As with Act V, Scene VIII, many editions of *Macbeth* have this scene also play through, unbroken, from the prior scene, rather than starting "Scene IX." A few editions combine all three scenes into a single, final Scene VII.

commanded any shred of loyalty at the end. But, as in all armed combat, there had still been a cost.

"Some must die," said Siward, well familiar with the price of warfare, "and yet, by these I see, so great a day as this is cheaply bought."

"Macduff is missing," Malcolm reminded him, "and your noble son."

Ross approached, and having been near enough to hear Malcolm's words, hesitated only briefly before addressing Siward with a heavy heart. "Your son, my Lord, has paid a soldier's debt. He lived until he was a *man* ... then, no sooner had his prowess been confirmed in the unflinching station where he fought ... like a man, he died."

Siward's face remained impassive, for the most part, when he asked, "Then he *is* dead?"

Ross nodded. "Aye, and brought off the field of battle." He placed a compassionate hand upon Siward's shoulder. "Your cause of sorrow must not be measured by his worth, for then it has no end."

Still stalwart, Siward asked. "Did he have his wounds on the front of him?"

"Aye, on the front."

With this, Siward's emotions flowed more freely, but they were as much relief and joy as they were sadness. "Why then, he is *God's* soldier! Had I as many sons as I have hairs, I would not wish them to a fairer death." He drew a deep breath, and settled into a quiet calm. "And so, his death knell is tolled."

Malcolm spoke up. "He's worth more sorrow, and that *I'll* spend for him." Many around the Prince of Cumberland nodded their agreement.

But Siward insisted, "He's worth no more; they say he departed well, and paid his score, and so, God is with him!" And then Siward's gaze was drawn past Malcolm, and in spite of the recent news, a victorious smile graced his lips. "Here comes newer comfort."

Malcolm and the others turned to see what Siward was looking upon, and several gasps escaped the throng.

A tired and bloody Macduff approached them, the English and Scottish soldiers parting before him ...

... and in his hands, he carried the head of Macbeth.

"Hail, King!" Macduff called as he stopped before Malcolm, "for so you are." He dropped Macbeth's head onto the ground. "Behold, where stands the usurper's cursed head; the time is *free*."

A wave of relief and pleasure passed through the crowd, English and Scottish alike.

Macduff gestured to the Thanes who surrounded Malcolm. "I see you compassed with your Kingdom's nobles, that speak my salutation in their minds; whose voices I desire aloud with mine: Hail, *King* of Scotland!"

Fists rose into the air as the crowd echoed together, "Hail, King of Scotland!"

Trumpets sounded and drums beat, but Malcolm – content, but not as filled with merriment as his supporters – waved them all to silence. It took a full minute, but eventually the King's first command was heeded.

"I shall not spend a large expense of time before I reckon with your devotions, and make myself properly even with you," Malcolm proclaimed. "My Thanes and kinsmen ... henceforth be *Earls* – the first that Scotland ever named in such an honor. What's more to do, which would be newly planted with the time, as calling home our exiled friends abroad that fled the snares of watchful tyranny, and producing for trial the cruel ministers of this dead butcher and his fiend-like Queen, who – as it is thought – by her own violent hands ended her life. This, and whatever other needs that call upon me, by the grace of God, I will perform in proper decorum, time, and place." He turned in a full circle as he concluded, "So thanks to *all* at once and to each one, whom I invite to see me crowned at Scone."

More trumpets, more drums, more calls of support and cries of comfort. For these words marked the end of the tyranny of Macbeth – Macbeth, once the loyal General, the Thane of Glamis, who fought for King and country rather than avarice and personal gain.

What had tainted such a man? Rumors abounded of his obsession with three sisters – witches he encountered, and who lured him into darkness with the secret desires buried deep within his own heart. And who among us lacked such desires, which most of us entombed and were never forced to face?

If such rumors were true, then thus concluded not only the oppression of Macbeth ...

... but also the tragedy of Macbeth.

The following literature and films were *invaluable* in my efforts to novelize *Macbeth*.

LITERATURE

The Riverside Shakespeare, 1974 edition*
The Yale Shakespeare, 1954 edition*
The Arden Shakespeare, 1985 edition
Asimov's Guide to Shakespeare, by Isaac Asimov
No Fear Shakespeare, by SparkNotes LLC
No Fear Shakespeare Graphic Novels, by Spark Publishing

FILMS

Great Performances: Macbeth, 2010*
Directed by Rupert Goold, starring Patrick Stewart.

A Performance of Macbeth, 1979*
Directed by Philip Casson, starring Ian McKellen.

Macbeth, 1971*
Directed by Roman Polanski, starring Jon Finch.

Macbeth, 1983
Directed by Jack Gold, starring Nicol Williamson.

Macbeth, 2006
Directed by Geoffrey Wright, starring Sam Worthington.

About the Author

CHRISTOPHER ANDREWS lives in California with his wife, Yvonne Isaak-Andrews, their beautiful daughter, Arianna, and their Pug, PJ. In addition to his duties as stay-at-home Dad, he is working on his next novels, and continues to work as an actor and screenwriter.

Excerpts from all of Christopher's novels can be found at www.ChristopherAndrews.com.

www.ingramcontent.com/pod-product-compliance
Lightning Source LLC
Chambersburg PA
CBHW020638110726
47899CB00002B/816